Dear Readers,

We're so excited to release

Bros. 47 R.O.N.I.N.! When we decided to develop a book series, we wanted to create stories kids our age would love. So we jam-packed our series with all of the cool things we love to read about—top secret plots, ninja fighters, ancient samurai weapons, and ultimate villains. We even have a lot in common with the main characters, Tom and Mitch, from our favorite desserts to our favorite bands. Because we love comics so much, we've included original comic book-style art—illustrated by an awesome comic book artist—in each book. We think it rocks, and we hope you do too!

Thanks for reading our series, and stay tuned for future episodes of Sprouse Bros. 47 R.O.N.I.N.!

Dylan Sprouse and Cole Sprouse

We would like to thank our dad,
Matt, and our manager, Josh, for
their constant support. Thanks also
to everyone at Dualstar and Simon & Schuster for all their hard work. Last,
but not least, thanks to all our friends
and fans—this is for you guys!
—Dylan Sprouse and Cole Sprouse

SIMON SPOTLIGHT
An imprint of Simon & Schuster Children's Publishing Division • 1230 Avenue of the Americas, New York, New York 10020

Manufactured in the United States of America • First Edition 10 9 8 7 6 5 4 3 2 1
ISBN-13: 978-1-4169-4785-1 • ISBN-10: 1-4169-4785-X
Library of Congress Catalog Card Number 2008920330

EPISODE 6 THE COMEBACK

by Kevin Ryan
with Dylan Sprouse and Cole Sprouse
illustrated by Shane L. Johnson

Simon Spotlight
New York London Toronto Sydney

Even a sheet of paper has two sides.

–Japanese proverb

PROLOGUE

CENTRAL PARK, NEW YORK CITY

Eight Years Ago

"Here we are, Mr. Hearn," Jin Chance said.

"Thank you, Jin . . . and you can call me Jack," he replied.

"Yes, Mr. Hearn," Jin responded with a smile.

It was their private joke. Jack had been trying to get his employee to call him by his first name for nearly ten years, but Jin never once did. Grinning, Jack decided he would keep trying.

Approximately ten years before, Jack had hired Jin Chance as a salesman in his computer networking division. Jack had immediately seen potential in the man, and not just as a salesman. After a few years, he recruited Jin to join R.O.N.I.N. as a member of Jack's own Cat's Claw Clan.

This was not a decision that Jack had made lightly.

R.O.N.I.N., or the Rogue Operative Network Inter-National organization, was dedicated to the global fight against evil wherever it might be found, and as such was highly secretive.

Over time, Jin became not only a trusted employee to Jack, but also a friend and a partner on a number of R.O.N.I.N. missions. He had been a great help in the weeks after Jack's wife, Madeline, died—practically running the company for months while Jack tended to his boys. The fact that he could rely on Jin was a great comfort, even now as he was beginning to get back to work.

Mitch and Tom were understandably having trouble adjusting to life without their beloved mother. They were just seven years old, and this loss had been the most painful experience they had ever faced as a family. Jack tried hard to fill Madeline's shoes, but it was an impossible task. He knew all he could do was promise to always be there for his kids, a promise he would strive the rest of his life to keep. In the months after Madeline passed away, Jack would put his sons to bed and watch them sleep, silently praying that nothing would ever take them away from him.

Since their mother's death, there were times when the boys were quiet for long periods of time, something that had never happened before. But today was obviously not one of those times, at least judging by the panicked phone call he received from their sitter.

Jin dropped him off at the 59th Street entrance to Central Park and went to park the car. Jack headed for the boys' favorite spot and soon spotted the large gray rocks he was sure to find them climbing.

As he got closer, he heard laughing—as well as panic-stricken cries.

"Come down! Come down!" a female voice shrieked.

Jack couldn't see Tom or Mitch, but it was their laughter he heard. That alone made him smile. It was the first time he'd heard them really laughing since Madeline died. Then Jack saw two blond heads popping up from behind the rocks.

He could also see Susan, the new sitter, pacing back and forth, glancing worriedly up at the rocks. Susan had been with them for about five days, and she had already called Jack at least a dozen times. After the incidents with the whipped cream, the skateboard, the stepladder, and the ceiling fan, he had a stern talk with the boys, which he thought would take care of their mischievous behavior.

Apparently not.

"Get down right now!" Susan yelled. "Your father will be here any minute and–"

Then she let out a scream, and Jack watched as both Mitch and Tom assumed handstand positions and attempted to walk down the rock upside down on their hands.

"Stop!" she ordered.

The twins leaped to their feet and smiled. "Which is it?" asked Tom.

"Yeah, do you want us to come down there or not?" Mitch put in.

"No more of this, just get down here without doing anything dangerous. And do it now!" she said angrily.

Jack was relieved when the boys started walking down normally. Then suddenly Tom stumbled and fell backward. Mitch grabbed him, and then both boys fell out of sight.

Jack started running but had taken only a few steps when the boys popped back up, laughing. Relieved, he forced back a smile and shouted, "Boys, get down here!"

Hearing him, the boys straightened up and climbed down. Jack approached the sitter. "I'm sorry, Susan," he said, as he smiled at the boys.

"You have no idea what they get up to!" Susan cried.

"I'll talk to them," Jack said, nonchalantly, not realizing that he was still smiling.

"Do you think this is funny?" she demanded.

"No, of course not," he said, trying to change his expression and—by the look on Susan's face—failing.

When Jack had first met her two weeks ago, she was a calm, serious graduate student at Columbia. Now she was still a serious graduate student, but calm . . . that was up for debate.

"This is why!" said Susan. "They know they can get away with anything and you'll think it's just a big joke."

Jack shook his head. "That's not true. I talked to them about the skateboard on the stairs, and the whipped cream on the neighbor's window—"

"And what good did it do? They just find other ways to try to kill themselves and torture me," she insisted.

“I’m sure I can straighten all of this out,” said Jack.

“Well, you can do it without me. Look, I’m sorry about what happened to your family, but I’m not cut out for this. I quit!”

“It hasn’t even been a week,” Jack protested.

“Well, it feels like a lot longer,” said Susan as she turned away.

“Wait . . . ,” Jack called, but Susan’s determined strides made it very clear that nothing could change her mind.

“Dad, we were just playing around,” Tom said. His earnest face made Jack smile. He rubbed his son’s head.

“I know that, but your playing around was getting a little out of hand,” he said.

“What if we apologize?” Mitch suggested.

“No, I don’t think that’s going to do any good this time,” Jack said.

“Sorry, Dad,” said Tom. “I guess you’ll have to stay home,” he added brightly.

At that moment Jack understood. For seven years the boys had their mother with them day and night. When they lost her, they got used to having their father around. And now that Jack had gone back to work, they had neither. Maybe Jack had started working again too soon. Yet he had responsibilities there, and to R.O.N.I.N. as well.

The Dragon—the leader of all the R.O.N.I.N. clans—needed Jack for a mission that would begin in less than two weeks. Would the boys be okay without him?

"Boys," he said, squatting down to look directly into their faces, "I would love to stay home, but I have to work. And I have other things to take care of. . . ." Jack paused for a moment, then added, "You'll understand when you get older."

Mitch and Tom nodded their heads, understanding as well as seven-year-olds could.

Just then Jin appeared. "Mr. Hearn, the meeting," he reminded his employer.

"Oh," Jack said, standing up. "These are my sons, Tom and Mitch. Tom, Mitch, this is Mr. Chance, the best salesman on my team."

"Cool name," said Mitch, as Jin smiled widely and shook the boys' hands.

Tom tugged on his dad's arm. "I'm hungry, Dad," he said. "Can I get a hot dog?"

"Sure," Jack replied, as he scanned the park for a hot dog vendor. Spotting one at the other end of a nearby tunnel, he asked Jin to watch the boys while he went to get the food.

"Two, with ketchup," he told the vendor, before pulling a few bills out of his wallet. Then, with the warm hot dogs in one hand, he headed back into the tunnel.

Suddenly Jack felt a sharp jab in his back. "Give me your wallet," a man's voice growled.

Jack didn't waste a second. Dropping the hot dogs, he turned his body toward his attacker and grabbed the man's wrist, performing a joint lock that caused him to yelp in pain and let go of what turned out to be a toy gun.

The attacker was clearly not expecting his victim to put up a fight, but Jack easily locked the man's arm against his back. Then Jack noticed a second attacker heading straight for them. Using the first robber as a shield, Jack pushed the other man back, then spun around to land a roundhouse kick to the man's jaw. The other man immediately fell to the ground.

The commotion brought two NYPD officers to the scene, and Jack's attackers were quickly handcuffed.

Jack looked up to see the wide-eyed, openmouthed faces of his sons, who for the first time had just seen their dad fight.

"Dad, you were awesome!" Tom cried as he and Mitch ran up to Jack.

"Dad," called Mitch proudly, "you kicked those guys'–"

"Sorry I dropped your hot dogs," Jack interrupted right on time, and they all burst out laughing.

"Are you okay, sir?" Jin asked. "I surmised that you were doing fine on your own, and I didn't want the boys to be harmed, so we stayed away."

"You were right. Thank you so much for keeping them safe," Jack replied. Just then his watch started beeping, and he and Jin exchanged glances. "The meeting," said Jack.

Then, as if reading his mind, Jin told Jack, "Sir, I could look after the children."

"Do you have any experience with children?" Jack asked, surprised but touched by the offer.

Jin shook his head. "None."

"Perfect. Experience with normal kids wouldn't do you any good anyway," said Jack, grinning. "I really appreciate it, Jin. I can take a cab to the meeting. If you could just get the boys home in one piece and keep an eye on things until I get back . . ."

"Don't worry, Mr. Hearn," Jin assured him. "Your boys will be fine." Then, turning to Mitch and Tom, he added, "Right, boys?"

"Yes," the boys immediately agreed.

The presentation went well, and Jack left the conference room with the largest order of his career. He was back in their East Side home by six. Immediately he saw that something was different. Actually, he *smelled* something different.

Someone was cooking.

It wasn't until that moment that Jack realized how long it had been since anyone had used the Hearns' state-of-the-art kitchen. Of course, he remembered the last meal—spaghetti and meatballs, the boys' favorite dish. Madeline had made it the night before she died. Since then, Jack and the boys had pretty much lived on takeout and pizza.

Heading for the kitchen, Jack saw the boys and Jin, who was hovering over the stove.

All heads turned when he entered.

"Dad," said Mitch, "Mr. Chance made dinner."

"Chili," Tom added, with his mouth full.

"Well, it smells delicious," Jack said.

"How'd your meeting go?" asked Mitch.

"Great. Made a big sale today. Jin, I'll have to fill you in later," Jack said.

"Very well," said Jin. "I'll say good-bye then."

"No, please stay. After all, you cooked," Jack pointed out.

Dinner was surprisingly normal. The boys had questions about how their dad had learned to fight and asked when they could start learning martial arts. They talked a lot about how Jin learned to cook as a chef in a Japanese restaurant.

As they finished their meal, Jack's phone beeped, indicating that he'd just received a text message. Jack opened his phone and scrolled to the message: TATSU was all it said. *Tatsu* was the Japanese word for dragon; duty was calling.

"Business, boys. Mr. Chance, you and I have a call to take," Jack said, getting up.

In Jack's home office, the two men waited for the phone to ring. When it did, Jack picked up immediately.

"Hello, Jack," said the voice on the other end. Jack had met the Dragon only once or twice in his life, and he'd spoken directly to him only rarely, when something urgent came up.

No one, not even the leaders of the R.O.N.I.N. clans, was certain of the Dragon's identity or whereabouts. Clan members met the Dragon at least once in their lives—during the R.O.N.I.N. initiation ceremony. And even that memory was clouded by the ritual hypnosis that protected both the identity of the Dragon and the location of Dragon Island.

And Jack himself knew only a handful of clan leaders. That secrecy was an important safeguard for the organization, ensuring that even if one clan was compromised, the vast majority of the others would remain safe.

"You can put Jin on the line," the Dragon said. Jack nodded to Jin, then placed the call on speakerphone.

"I am concerned about you, Jack," the Dragon continued, "and about your clan. Your boys are still young. I know that you can handle yourself, but there have been signs of trouble. A few of our clans have gone silent. And your wife's sudden death . . ."

Taken aback at this insinuation, Jack became defensive. "There was no sign that her death was anything but natural." If it hadn't been natural, that would mean he had failed his beloved, and he wasn't about to admit that to anyone. But deep down he knew there was nothing natural about a woman of thirty-four suddenly dying of a brain aneurysm. And yet there had been no indication of foul play, and he thought they were all better off letting it go.

"Nevertheless, I feel you need qualified assistance, additional security for your sons," the Dragon said.

"What do you have in mind?" asked Jack. He was intrigued by the concern that the Dragon was showing for his family, and he trusted him, but the last thing his family needed was for his sons to be sent off into seclusion somewhere. They needed to stick together, and he was prepared to fight for that.

"Jack, I want you to hire Jin," the Dragon said.

"But he already works for me."

"As a guardian for your sons," the Dragon went on evenly.

Jack had to admit, he was relieved he didn't have to fight with the Dragon about keeping the boys at home with him. This seemed like a great proposition—for him. But as he looked at Jin, an expression Jack didn't recognize flickered across the man's face. Was it resentment? Was it anger? He couldn't tell. . . .

"But he is one of my top employees. I can't ask him to leave a promising career for—"

"For the greater good of the R.O.N.I.N.? Jin, how do you feel about sacrificing yourself for the safety and sanctity of future R.O.N.I.N. leaders?" the Dragon asked.

"I will serve where I am needed," answered Jin calmly, and Jack saw it again, a slight squint to Jin's eye, an odd set to his mouth, and then it was gone. For years Jack would assume it had been a natural reaction to being asked to make a personal sacrifice. But he also couldn't help wondering about that expression, because it seemed so out of place on Jin's face—like it belonged to someone else, someone Jack didn't know.

"Very well, it's settled. Good-bye," the Dragon said, and he hung up.

"Jin, I don't know what to say," said Jack.

"No words are necessary. We have our orders, and I have a new job," Jin stated matter-of-factly. And the two men never discussed this transition again.

CHAPTER 1

THE RAKURAI, PACIFIC OCEAN

Present Day

"Dad!" Mitch and Tom called out at once.

Jack Hearn smiled wearily at his sons. He was relieved to finally be able to reveal himself to them, but how were they going to respond to him after he'd just attacked their beloved guardian? Would they think *he* was the enemy? Would they fear him?

Tom and Mitch just stood at a distance, completely dumbfounded and confused.

"Dad," Tom began, "you just–"

"You killed Mr. Chance," said Mitch. Then he demanded angrily, "Who are you? Have you been brainwashed?"

Jack wished that he could've spared them from seeing what had just happened. But he didn't have a choice.

"I'm sorry, boys. I know this is difficult, but you

have to believe me when I tell you that Jin Chance was a traitor to the family," he told them.

"But why? How?" said Tom.

"That's not possible," Mitch added.

"It's true. I wouldn't have done it unless I had to," he said. Suddenly he felt the toll of the day weigh on him. He realized he was exhausted, and his left arm was starting to throb from the gash Jin had branded him with. All Jack wanted to do was sleep, but he couldn't, not until his boys knew he was not to be feared.

"Boys, I will explain everything. For now, I want you to know that I haven't changed. I haven't been brainwashed or compromised in any way. I did what I needed to do to protect you, our family, and our clan. Please believe me."

Then Jack held out his arms. For a moment he was afraid they would turn away from him.

Waiting there like that, the moment seemed to last an eternity. But suddenly Tom and Mitch both bounded toward him and hugged him so tightly he had trouble catching his breath. "We thought you were dead," Tom said, trying to stifle his tears.

"I'm sorry. I'm so sorry. I tried to get to you, tried to tell you, but . . . well, things got a little complicated."

The boys continued to hug their father until a low, rumbling sound made them look up. Vane Island had literally crumbled to pieces: rocks, debris, all lay strewn across the salty waters, while the rest of the island plunged to the depths of the ocean floor.

"Hey, look," Tom said suddenly, pointing to the sky.

The sound of beating helicopter rotors had brought their gaze up just in time to watch Vane flee the scene.

"I knew he'd have an escape plan," said Jack.

"Dad," Tom began, looking back at his father, "how do you know that Mr. Chance–"

Jack held up his hand. "I know you boys have a hundred questions for me, and I promise I'll answer them all as best as I can, but for now I want you to get some rest. Our mission is not complete, not by a long shot, and we all need to be at our best."

"Then it would be best if you stop bleeding all over the deck," a female voice declared in Russian-accented English. Jack, Tom, and Mitch turned to see the beautiful Nadia Petrova, who had also been watching Vane's helicopter take off.

"Boys, you haven't introduced me to your . . . friend," Jack said, staring at the stranger intently.

"This is Nadia," said Mitch. "She, uh, helped us get out of Vane's tower and into his prison so we could free everyone."

"And your sons got me off this island of doom," Nadia added, shaking her head.

"Yes, I saw you on the island with Vane," Jack noted.

"Looks like your boss left without you."

"He was not very nice boss," said Nadia, with marked disdain in her voice. Then she looked down at Jack's arm. "I have basic medic training. I look at that later."

Jack was unsure what sort of medical training Nadia might have, especially since he had only seen Vanc's assistants make drinks and run errands. But he agreed to let her help him.

Once the helicopter had vanished from sight, Nadia retired back downstairs to her cabin. It was getting dark, and everyone was looking forward to a peaceful night's sleep.

Just then Inoshiro Matsu appeared. "Jack, a word with you, please," he requested.

"I'm sorry, Inoshiro," Jack replied, "but I'm done keeping secrets. Anything you have to say can be said in front of my boys. They're R.O.N.I.N. now too, and I believe they've proven themselves quite worthy of any inside information we may have."

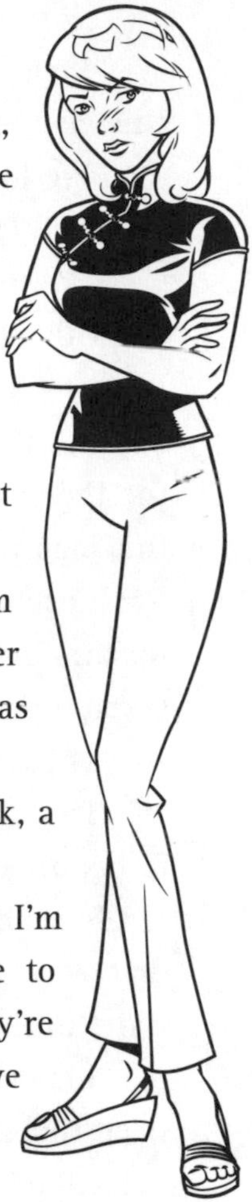

"Very well. We need to set a course for the ship. I discovered what I think is a map drawn by Dr. Gensai," Inoshiro said, holding out the map. "It seems the previous crew was following the map's course."

"Boys," Jack asked nervously, "where did you find this map? Why were you following it?"

"We have stuff to fill you in on too, Dad," replied Mitch. "We were on the hunt for Dragon Island."

"How do you know—you know what, we'll talk about all of this later. Inoshiro, my boys are dead on. We need to go to Dragon Island." Seeing Inoshiro's reaction, he added, "Trust me on this one. Dr. Gensai can give you the the exact coordinates; no need to try and decipher this map when we have its author on board."

Inoshiro nodded. "I will talk to him, and then arrange for him and his daughter, as well as Ms. Petrova, to be taken to Tokyo."

"Is Laura okay?" Tom asked Inoshiro.

"Laura's fine," Inoshiro assured him. "She and her father are catching up with each other."

Tom and Mitch breathed a sigh of relief. Knowing that Laura was taken care of, the boys led Jack down the stairs to their cabins.

"I have an extra bunk in my cabin, Dad, so you can sleep there," Tom offered. "But we are *way* too tired to sleep. We have to know everything!"

"Whoa, speak for yourself, Tom. I could use a few hours of sleep before we get into everything," said Mitch, yawning. Then he gave his father a hug good night, went into his cabin, and flopped down heavily on his bunk.

"It's really good to have you back, Dad. See you in the morning." And that was the last thing Mitch said before falling asleep.

When they got to Tom's cabin, Tom gave his dad another hug before climbing into bed.

"Any chance you'll dish the details without Mitch?"

"Nope." Jack laughed, patting his son on the back.

It was good to hear his dad's voice again. For the first time in a long while, Tom felt safe.

"I'm really glad you're back, Dad," said Tom, as he closed his eyes.

As Tom drifted off to sleep, Jack sat in the dim light watching his son's chest rise and fall peacefully. His thoughts drifted back to a time when things were simpler, when the boys had normal lives; when they went to school, played video games, and were tucked safely in their beds at night by their mother. That's the way it should *still* be, he thought. Then he recalled, with anger, that for the last eight years, the very person he'd depended on to take over their mother's daily routine and protect his sons from harm was the person who had been plotting all along to destroy them.

He silently renewed the promise he had made a long time ago: He would never leave their side again, no matter what it took.

CHAPTER 2

Jack knocked on Nadia's cabin door. She opened the door, stared for a moment, and gestured for him to take a seat in the small but brightly lit room. Then she reached into a drawer for a pair of scissors.

She began to cut through the sleeve of his ninja kimono, revealing a five-inch gash that extended to the top of his forearm.

"He was quite a fighter," Nadia observed, referring to Jin Chance.

"Our business takes its toll," Jack replied.

"And that business is . . . ?"

"Electronics and computers."

"Ah. I did not know the computer business is so dangerous," she said, as she cleaned the wound.

"Every line of work has its downside," noted Jack.

"Well, your sons will do well in this business," she told him. She held up a box of butterfly bandages. "You need stitches, but these will do for now."

"Fine, thanks," Jack said with a shrug. Then he asked, "Why are you being so nice to a total stranger?"

"I have my reasons . . . and I owe something to your boys," Nadia replied. She gently applied some antibiotic ointment to the wound, then deftly wrapped his arm with gauze and closed it with three large bandages. It seemed as though she had done this many times before.

"Where did you learn to do this?" he asked her.

"I have a brother," she answered, and didn't offer any further explanation before quickly adding, "Okay, I'm done."

"Well, thanks," Jack said, before standing to leave her cabin. He admired Nadia's handiwork for a moment before heading up to the bridge, where he found Inoshiro.

"Here's some clothing. I'm sure you want to get out of that outfit." Inoshiro held out a small pile of men's shirts and pants. "Get some rest, Jack. We are on course."

Jack didn't argue. When he returned to Tom's room, the boy was still asleep. He was glad to finally rid himself of the black ninja suit, which he threw into the garbage before heading to bed. Jack lay awake for a while, as a million thoughts ran through his head. Whatever happened tomorrow, he was grateful his sons were with him now.

A few hours later Jack awoke, feeling better than he

had in weeks. He was at last strong enough to explain everything to his sons, and he considered waking them up when he heard someone knocking softly on the door.

Jack opened the door to see Mitch, wearing a big grin on his face.

"Rise and shine, Dad," he said. "You've got a lot of explaining to do."

Jack chuckled as he hugged his son tightly. Then Mitch released himself and began yanking the covers off his brother's bed.

"Stop," Tom mumbled sleepily.

"Wake up, Tom. Dad's here, and he's ready to talk."

Tom shot up in bed and broke into a smile, even though his eyes were closed until Mitch hit him with a pillow. "Okay, okay," Tom said. "I'm awake. I'm just so tired."

Jack took a deep breath. "I'm sorry for what you boys have been through. I'm sorry for what you saw yesterday, for bringing that man into our lives, and for having been gone so long. I've missed telling you all about R.O.N.I.N., our clan—"

"It's okay, Dad, really," Mitch interrupted. "It's been rough, but nothing we couldn't handle, right, Tom?"

Tom nodded. "Yeah. We're just glad you're here. We have so much to tell you, and we're finally back on course to Dragon Island—"

"Yeah, how do you know about Dragon Island?"

Jack asked, more concerned than curious.

"That's where the sacred scroll is kept," explained Tom, "and probably why Dr. Gensai was taken, but what we don't know–"

"Wait, first things first," Jack said, taking a deep breath. "Let me fill you in on what you don't know–well, as much as I can–and we'll go from there. Otherwise I have a feeling things are going to get way too confusing. . . . So, remember the night of the Citywide Science Fair last year? Well, Mr. Ting and I had arranged to meet there. We were worried because we were each having trouble reaching some of the clan leaders we knew. Something just felt wrong."

"Yeah," Tom added, "Laura said she saw you guys talking that night–she said that her dad bowed to you or something. Whoa, that feels so long ago–it was before we even knew Laura as anything but geek squad competition for Mitch and his science projects."

"Competition? This year won't even be a contest. She's going down," Mitch exclaimed.

Tom grinned. "Oh, give it up, bro." Then, turning to their dad, he said, "Sorry, Dad, Mitch has developed a bit of an imagination since you've been gone. Tell us what happened next."

"Well, we said good night that evening and vowed to keep a close watch on the situation and keep each other posted on any strange or unorthodox occurrences. Things seemed to be okay for a while after that. But then, I was on my way to the airport to go to Los Angeles for that last business trip when I was captured," Jack said.

"Was it supposed to be a real business trip?" asked Mitch.

"Yes, I had a meeting with an engineering group in Silicon Valley. But I also wanted to track down a clan leader who'd gone silent. I was on my way to the airport when I got the call."

侍

NEW YORK CITY

Ten Weeks Ago

Jack pulled away from the curb. As usual, he had left too late and was now in a rush. Mainly he was frustrated with himself for missing the boys that morning–they'd left for school early, and he hadn't gotten a chance to say good-bye.

Checking his watch, Jack saw that it was nearly nine. He could still make his flight if there were no major tie-ups on the way to JFK Airport. He had nearly reached the Midtown Tunnel when his cell phone rang. The caller ID indicated that the call was coming from the boys' school. For a moment he considered not answering. It was probably another request for help with one of the school's many fund-raisers.

Just in case, Jack hit send. "Jack Hearn here."

"Mr. Hearn, this is Cindy Latchford from your sons' school," she said. He didn't recognize the name, but that didn't mean much. He was sure that Jin knew her.

"Yes?" Jack said.

"I'm the school nurse," she said.

Jack suddenly didn't like her tone of voice. Something was wrong, he could tell. "What is it?" he asked sharply.

"There's been an accident. Both Mitchell and Thomas were hurt," she told him.

"Hurt? How?" Jack demanded.

"There was some scaffolding set up for some construction work . . . and part of it collapsed. . . ."

Jack brought the car to a screeching halt. "What's their condition?"

"I'm afraid I don't know. The ambulance just left for the hospital."

As she gave Jack the name of the hospital, he was already in motion, making a sharp U-turn. His heart was thundering in his chest as he headed uptown. Given the number of red lights he ran, it was a small miracle that he didn't get stopped by the police.

He reached the hospital and drove the car into the underground parking garage. Pulling up to the stop sign near the attendant's office, he jumped out of the car and frantically looked for an attendant, but no one was there.

"Anyone here?" he called out.

Just then he heard a familiar voice. "Jack?"

Jack turned around to see Roy Ting. "Hey, Roy, what are you doing here?"

"I got a call from my daughter's school," Ting said. "Laura is in the hospital. She was on a field trip to the U.N. and there was an accident."

Suddenly Jack's heart sank. He realized that their meeting was not a coincidence. It was a setup. They'd been had.

"Roy," Jack whispered, still searching the garage for hints. "Our kids are fine. It's us we should worry about . . . and we need to get out of here now. Run for it."

A shuffle clued Jack in to a large, hulking man standing in front of the exit. He was extremely muscular and looked to be almost seven feet tall. He was wearing a skintight suit that was at least two sizes too small for him.

"Too late to run," the giant bellowed.

"Who are you?" Jack demanded, scanning the underground lot for a way out.

"You can call me 'sir,'" the man said.

"That's not likely," said Roy.

The man shrugged in response. "The good news is

that your children are fine. The bad news is that *you* are in a bit of trouble."

"That's doubtful," Jack retorted. "I think you're the one in trouble."

The man smiled. "Well then, it's a good thing I brought friends."

Suddenly, half a dozen men appeared from behind cars and corners. Ninjas, Jack realized. And they were good—neither he nor Roy had seen nor heard them in all the time they'd been standing there.

Without saying anything to each other, Jack and Roy assumed back-to-back fighting stances. The ninjas began to circle them.

"You've made it a bit more interesting, but we're still walking out of here," Jack said.

"We can't say the same for you and your friends," added Roy.

The big man smiled again and simply raised one hand. Jack braced himself for an attack from six well-trained men. Instead the ninjas each pulled out small tubes, brought them to their mouths, and aimed them at their prey.

"Darts!" Jack said to Roy as he ducked instinctively, but it was too late. Three darts struck him in the chest, and his legs immediately felt like rubber; the room seemed to bend and stretch around him. Jack leaned backward and found a moment of support as he bumped against Roy, but the poison worked quickly. Within seconds Jack felt the ground rush up at him as darkness swallowed him.

CHAPTER 3

THE RAKURAI, PACIFIC OCEAN

Present Day

"When we didn't hear from you for a week, Mr. Chance told us you were busy, but that you had checked in with him," Tom said.

"And after two weeks, we started to really worry," Mitch continued. "You'd never been out of touch for so long. No calls, no e-mails, no text messages."

"But Mr. Chance told us everything was okay, and we had no reason not to believe him," said Tom, shaking his head. "If we'd suspected something was up, maybe . . ."

"You never suspected him because you had no reason to," said Jack, "because I brought him into our house. And I never suspected him myself, not even when I was sitting in a cell. . . ."

NEW YORK CITY

Ten Weeks Ago

Jack awoke slowly. His mind told him to leap up, to escape, but his body would not cooperate. He felt as though weights were pressing down on his chest and his arms and legs were made of lead. He could barely open his eyes, and when he finally did, all he saw was a gray concrete floor.

After a while he could move enough to lift his head. Even though Jack had trouble focusing, it looked like he was in some kind of square metal shed, with sides about a dozen feet long and ten feet high. Dim light squeezed in through a gate on one side. It had thick metal rods extending from top to bottom, and a heavy-duty lock attached.

"Roy, are you there?" Jack called out, finally coming to his senses.

"Yes, Jack," Roy replied weakly. "Are you okay?"

"Yeah," Jack said. "I'll be better as soon as I can stand up and think of a way out of here."

Jack didn't know if they were alone, but as far as he was concerned, anyone who might be listening would already assume they would try to escape. Little by little, he willed his body to start working again. Twenty minutes later he was on his feet, leaning against the metal wall of his cage for support.

He couldn't see Roy's cell but figured it wasn't more than ten feet away, based on the sound of Roy's voice. Jack heard Roy try to pull himself to his feet. From what he could see through his gate, their cells were on one end of a giant, vacant warehouse—two small sheds in a large, nearly empty space.

Jack tested the walls of the cell. They were solid and securely bolted to the floor. He examined the lock. If he had something small enough to pick it with, there might be hope. Jack went through the pockets of his suit. He still had his wallet, but his pen, PDA, and Pocket Pal mini tool kit were missing.

The cell contained the prison basics: a cot, a sink, and a toilet. There was nothing he could use to pick the lock. Whoever had kidnapped them knew what they were doing.

"Anything we can use, Roy?" Jack called out hopefully.

"Nothing. Our jailer has been very thorough," Roy answered, this time sounding a little stronger.

Well, it made sense. The whole operation seemed to have been well-planned. Jack could hear the sound of waves outside, and he guessed they were on the waterfront—probably in one of the many warehouses on the west side of Manhattan. There were windows near the ceiling of the building, but they were at least twenty feet up and showed him nothing but sky.

A few minutes later Jack heard movement outside. Then he saw a door open at the other end of the warehouse. Forcing himself to relax, he held on to the gate and waited. He immediately recognized the seven-foot-tall brute they had seen in the parking garage.

As the man got closer, he gave his prisoners a sneering smile. "How are you feeling?" he asked sarcastically.

Jack mumbled something under his breath.

"What's that, Jack?" the man asked.

Jack mumbled again, and the man stepped closer to look him over. "I know those drugs can be kind of rough," he said with a chuckle. "Don't worry. You'll be yourself by tonight." Then he leaned in closer and added, "Of course, the headache will last for days."

That was when Jack struck. His hand flew out and caught the giant square in the jaw. His hand still tingling from the punch, Jack saw the man's head turn sharply. Their kidnapper stumbled backward, but not quite far enough to end up within Roy's reach. That might have given them a chance.

On the other hand, Jack was satisfied that the man would be feeling *that* for days. The thug recovered quickly, wiped his mouth, and brought up blood on his hand. "You're going to pay for that," he spat.

"Why don't you come in here and collect?" Jack challenged.

The large man seemed to be considering the challenge for a moment, but then he smiled. "Nice try, but I'll make you pay from out here."

"Mr. Maldeen, that is no way to talk to our guests," said a voice.

Jack looked past the brute to see a man in a business suit walking toward them. He was also tall and muscular, though not as bulky as Maldeen. And this man had a completely shaven head. He was also familiar.

"Hello, Julian," Roy said, and Jack realized that the newcomer was Julian Vane. Jack knew that Vane had started his career at Ting's company, Ting Microsystems. Vane and Roy Ting had once been great friends, until Vane stole a piece of computer hardware Ting had developed—a disk controller with an intelligent caching algorithm that sped up access to data, effectively doubling the hard drive's throughput. This was particularly beneficial for large database applications. Vane claimed sole ownership of the patent for the controller, then made millions selling the device to major corporations.

That money had become the seed of Vane's now great fortune. In the business world, the wealthy financier was known to stop at nothing to get what he desired.

"What do you want with us?" Jack demanded.

Vane feigned surprise. "My, my, my, such a friendly greeting," he said smoothly. "I apologize for your current accommodations, Jack, but I promise you'll soon be in paradise."

"What good are we to you locked up?" Roy asked.

Vane laughed. "Don't flatter yourselves. You are only pawns in a much larger plan." Then he glanced over at Maldeen, who glared at Jack while wiping his bleeding lip. "Go take care of yourself, Maldeen."

Turning back to Jack, Vane continued, "I would appreciate it if you went a bit easier on the staff in the future. In the meantime, if there's anything you need—"

"A key for this lock would be good," Jack shot back.

Vane smiled. "Anything within reason. Perhaps some books, something to keep yourselves occupied? One of the guards will be along shortly. Let him know what you'd like and I'll see that you get it. We will move you soon enough, and I promise you something much more comfortable." And with that Vane took his exit.

"How soon is 'soon enough'?" Jack said to Roy once Vane had left.

"Whenever it is, that will be our chance to escape," answered Roy.

"Sure, but it could be days, weeks, or . . ." Jack's voice trailed off, and he combed his fingers through his hair as he thought of his sons. What would Jin tell them?

Vane stayed away for the next two days, keeping his prisoners in unbearable suspense.

Finally he made an appearance. "I'll be moving you next week. And before you waste any time planning your big escape during transit, you should know that we'll be using the darts again to make sure you're cooperative."

Jack's face didn't betray his disappointment as he gripped the bars of the cell gate tightly. The drugs in the darts were strong; he and Roy could wake up on the other side of the world when the drugs wore off.

"On the plus side," Vane continued, "the accommodations will be more sophisticated—and *much* more secure. You can prepare for a long stay."

"Why don't you just tell us what you want? Maybe we can help you," Jack offered desperately.

"I tell you what, we'll have a nice long talk when you reach your new home," Vane replied. "Oh, and you will have something else to look forward to. I'm going to see to it that your children join you."

At that moment something inside Jack snapped. He reached out for Vane, missing by inches. Still, the man was startled, and for a moment Jack saw a flicker of rage cross his face.

Jack wished he could have gotten at least one shot in with Vane, like he had with Maldeen. It wouldn't have really helped their situation; in fact, it probably would have made it worse. But it would have made him feel a thousand times better. After a moment, Vane turned to go. "I will see you soon, gentlemen," he said, and left the warehouse.

"Roy, we have to get out of here, right now," Jack whispered urgently.

"Any ideas as to how?"

"Not one. But we definitely have a deadline."

CHAPTER 4

THE RAKURAI, PACIFIC OCEAN

Present Day

It was dawn, the most beautiful time of day to be out sailing the open seas. The red and orange hues of the morning sunlight filled the horizon as the sun rose above the water. As he sat with his sons, Jack could hear voices in the hallway. He also heard a faint flapping noise off in the distance that seemed to be growing louder.

Seconds later Inoshiro Matsu knocked on Jack's cabin door. "Jack, come up to the deck. Bring your sons."

The three of them went up to the deck, where Laura and Roy Ting had already gathered.

The boys hugged Laura. "Hey!" said Tom.

"It's been so surreal having my dad back," Laura replied happily. "We were up almost all night talking. What about you guys? I can't believe your dad was the black ninja . . . and what happened with Mr. Chance?"

Tom and Mitch filled her in on what Jack had told them so far. Laura shook her head in disbelief at the news of Jin Chance's betrayal. "And see," she added, "I knew everything Vane told us on that island was a lie; Maldeen has been working for him this whole time."

"You had that right. Though, for the record, we were only *pretending* to listen to him, remember? Anyway," Mitch said seriously, "with Dr. Gensai's help, we're now headed directly for Dragon Island—"

Mitch was interrupted by a yelp from Laura, who had just spotted Emiko Gensai on the deck.

"Sorry, Mitch, I really want to hear the rest of the stuff your father told you, but with all the fighting and everything, Emiko and I haven't had a second to catch up. I want to make sure she's all right."

And with that, Laura bolted over to Emiko to give her a proper welcome-back hug. Tom and Mitch followed.

Emiko had had a rough few weeks. She'd been kidnapped and imprisoned by Vane. Then he'd forced her to create avatars, images of various important people, to fool others into thinking they were following the orders of their higher-ups, when in fact they were carrying out Vane's evil plans.

Emiko's dad, Dr. Hideki Gensai, had also appeared on deck, and joined Jack, Roy, and Inoshiro.

In the excitement of catching up with Emiko, Tom,

Mitch, and Laura didn't notice Kunio Matsu, leaning against the railing of the deck. After a few minutes, Tom suddenly met Kunio's gaze and stopped talking midsentence, which caused the others to turn and look at Kunio. They were all unsure of how to behave. After all, it was because of Kunio that so many of their loved ones had been in danger in the first place, but in the end, he was the reason they were all still alive. . . .

Just then, the flapping noise, which had started off as a faint hum, grew into a loud, frantic drumming from up above. One by one, they all looked up to the sky. A helicopter was approaching the ship, preparing to land.

"Please tell me that's not Vane's chopper?" Jack asked Inoshiro nervously.

"No, thankfully. That would be my daughter, Nikki," he answered, grinning broadly.

"Oh, good," said Jack, breathing a sigh of relief. "I'm not ready for another fight, not yet."

The helicopter touched down on the small landing area at the rear of the ship. Seconds later the door swung open, and Nikki jumped out. She immediately ran toward her father, who pulled her into a tight hug. "Father, I thought you were–"

"I am fine, my daughter," Inoshiro said.

"Hi, Nikki," said a voice from behind them.

Nikki looked up to see Kunio. Her expression

quickly changed, and she began to lash out in anger at her cousin. "You . . . ," she began to say as she took a step toward Kunio.

But Inoshiro took hold of Nikki's arm. "No, Nikki," he said gently.

"Father, he . . . he was working with Vane," Nikki protested. "He kidnapped one of my students—"

"I know. I know everything. Kunio has made some mistakes, but, like you, he thought he was operating on my orders. Vane created an elaborate lie, using the same graphics program to fool both of you."

"He did not fool me," Nikki replied defensively.

But Inoshiro did not acknowledge this remark. "We mustn't turn against each other," he continued. "Kunio is a loyal member of our family. Vane is the enemy."

After fiercely staring Kunio down for what must have felt like ages, Nikki finally relented. "Fine. As you wish," she replied, though she had trouble accepting that as an excuse. Hadn't she been able to tell the difference between her real father and an avatar? Wasn't she the one who put out the *doujinshi* to try to stop Vane?

Inoshiro nodded. "Good. Now, it's time for Dr. Gensai, Emiko, and Ms. Petrova to say good-bye and board the helicopter. Jack, if you don't mind getting Ms. Petrova . . ."

Turning her back on Kunio, Nikki rushed over to

greet the others as they all said good-bye to Emiko and her father.

Jack ushered Nadia up to the landing area. "This helicopter will bring you to Japan. There will be people there to help you."

"No," Nadia said firmly.

Jack was taken aback. "What do you mean, no?"

"I will not go to Japan. I stay with you and your sons," Nadia replied.

"I'm sorry, but you can't," Jack told her.

"What are you going to do, force me?" she answered. "I have no passport, no papers, and I don't want to go to Japan. I'm not going to trust strangers in strange country. I'm not sure I trust you. But I do trust your boys, and I will stay with them, thank you."

For a moment Jack was speechless. He hadn't counted on any resistance from Nadia.

"So, what would you like to do?" he finally asked.

"You are from America; I would like to go there. Whoever you are, and whatever your business is, I think you can help me."

Jack sighed in frustration. He looked to his boys, who were grinning from ear to ear. They seemed to really be enjoying the idea that a tall, beautiful, blond model was so attached to them. And what they enjoyed even more was that in this face-off between model and special agent, their dad seemed unable to win.

"Is there anything else you'd like?" Jack asked, with a touch of sarcasm.

"No, not at the moment," Nadia said.

Jack turned to Inoshiro, expecting him to insist that Nadia leave. Instead he agreed that Nadia could stay.

Throwing his hands up in defeat, Jack turned back to Nadia. "Okay, you can stay, but there are no guarantees for your safety. And there are certain things we can't discuss in front of you, so if you don't mind going back to your cabin now, we'd appreciate it."

"Okay," Nadia agreed, before slipping back down.

As Nadia climbed the steps back down to her cabin, Emiko and her father waved one last time and boarded the helicopter. And just like that, they were on their way back to Tokyo.

After watching the helicopter disappear in the distance, the boys turned their attention back to their father, eager for him to continue his tale.

"I was telling the boys about being captured by Vane in New York," Jack said, looking at Roy. The two of them were sitting with Tom, Mitch, Laura, Inoshiro, Nikki, and Kunio.

"Ah, yes, I still remember those powerful drugs," said Roy, shaking his head.

"So we both knew we needed to get out, but the walls of the cells were solid, and we had nothing to pick the lock with," Jack said. "And we were running out of time before Vane took us somewhere else."

"What did you do?" Tom asked.

"We improvised," replied Jack.

NEW YORK CITY

Seven Weeks Ago

Jack waited impatiently for Vane to make his move. Now that he and Roy had come up with an escape plan, time seemed to be moving at an absolute crawl. Finally, one day he saw the door open, and one of Vane's guards entered the room.

Dressed in full black ninja attire, the large guard pushed what looked like a hotel room service cart, compete with white tablecloth, through the warehouse. The night's dinner was from Bombay, an excellent Indian restaurant in the city. It was one of his and his sons' favorite places, but if all went according to plan, he and Roy wouldn't even get to taste the food.

Jack positioned himself by the door of his cell.

Sensing possible danger, the ninja stopped short, feet away from the cell's gate. "Against the wall," the guard ordered his prisoner.

Jack knew he had to find a way to break the ninja down in order for this plan to work. And the best way to break anybody down is to make them doubt themselves. "Vane said he's not happy with your work," Jack remarked in a casual tone.

The ninja tried to resist the bait, but he was too curious and fearful of Vane to succeed. "Oh, yeah?" he asked. "What'd he tell you?"

"He said he doesn't like the way you fold our napkins," Jack replied.

The ninja huffed up to the gate of Jack's cell in a rage. "You think you're funny, Hearn? Well, you won't be laughing when you find out what Vane has planned for you and your sons."

Angered, Jack reached through the bars of the gate. Laughing, the ninja quickly stepped back.

"What's he planning?" Jack demanded.

"Something special," the guard retorted. "Don't worry, it's going to be quite a vacation for you. Some might even call it an island paradise." Then he laughed even harder.

At that moment Jack had an idea. "An island paradise, huh?" he said, hoping to get more information from the guard. "Hope it's someplace like Tahiti. I've always wanted to bring my boys there."

"Close enough. It's in the Pacific . . . far, far way from home–" The guard stopped himself. "Hey, I know what you're doing, but you're not getting another word out of me!"

"I'm not so sure about that. There may be a few choice words you'll be uttering soon," said Jack.

"What do you mean?"

"Well, you're about to be in a lot of pain."

"Ha. You can't touch me," the ninja replied arrogantly.

"No . . . but he can," Jack said, just as Roy slammed one of the wooden legs from his bed in between the cells, hitting the ninja square on his shoulder. It wasn't enough to take him down, but it did cause him to spin around, making him an excellent target for Roy's next shot, which caught him right in the forehead.

The ninja remained on his feet, but he staggered backward to catch his balance and fell right into Jack's swinging fist. Then, reaching out with his left hand, Jack grabbed the ninja's robe to control his fall. He needed the man's body within reach.

The ninja was out cold, and Jack pulled him closer to sift through his pockets. "Great . . . no keys," he said loudly. Vane may have been a thief and a liar, but he wasn't an idiot. They needed a new plan.

"Is there anything in there you can use?" Roy asked. Jack pulled out a tube and two darts from the ninja's sleeve—the same ones that were used on them in the parking garage. He got to work immediately on the lock. It was tricky; he had to use both steel points to work the mechanism's tumblers, but after fifteen minutes his gate opened.

So far so good, Jack thought, but there was still a long way to go before they were home free. Jack passed the darts to Roy, who didn't waste a second getting started on his lock.

Jack found two more darts on the guard and stuck them into the ninja's arms, ensuring that the man would be out for a few more hours while they made their escape. Jack quickly switched clothes with the ninja and then dragged him over to the far corner of the expansive warehouse, hiding the man behind a tall stack of wooden crates.

"How's it going with that lock?" Jack called to Roy.

"Slowly," Roy replied, frustration in his voice.

Jack scaled the boxes at the other side of the warehouse until he could reach and open a window. He drank in the crisp, fresh air as he looked at the Hudson River below him. He didn't think they'd have a problem escaping the warehouse through this window—as long as they did it quickly and without being seen.

Jack hurried back to Roy's cell. "Roy, we have to go. How much longer do you think you'll need?"

"It's no use, Jack," said Roy dejectedly. "The point of one of the darts broke off inside the lock."

"No . . . No, no, no . . ." Jack repeated pointlessly. He attempted to unlock Roy's gate himself, but his friend was right: It was no use. Given unlimited time and the right tools, he might be able to remove the steel point from the lock and open it. But he had neither tools nor time. The next guard shift would start in less than five minutes—and if the guards were wise enough to notice that their fellow worker had not yet returned from serving dinner, Jack and Roy might find themselves with even less time.

"Get out of here, Jack, we don't have time," Roy insisted.

"No, I won't leave you," Jack replied instinctively, even though in his heart he knew that he had to go.

"We have a chance if you can get out of here. Our children have a chance."

Jack knew that Roy was right. The children were the most important people in this, and it was up to him to save his boys and Roy's daughter. "You're right," Jack said grimly. "I'll come back for you as soon as I can."

Just as he turned toward the exit, another guard

came in. Thinking quickly, Jack dove down to the ground next to his old cell and just lay there as if he were passed out. He could hear the footsteps getting closer, until he could feel the guard peering down on him from above.

"Mr. Maldeen!" the new guard yelled. "You better get in here!"

A few seconds later Maldeen came running in. He shook Jack until he stirred.

"Spellman," Maldeen said. "What happened?"

Jack got up slowly and pointed to the wooden bed legs that had fallen to the ground. "The Hearn guy hit me with those. He got away!" he groaned, trying to emulate Spellman's voice. He didn't think he did a particularly good job, but Maldeen bought it.

"I've had it with you, Spellman," Maldeen said, looking into Jack's cell. "If we lost him, we'll all be in serious trouble. I can try to hold Vane off, but it won't last long. Go find him–NOW! If Jack Hearn isn't back before Vane gets here, you're a dead man!"

Jack nodded and pointed to the open window above them as more ninjas streamed into the facility.

"I'll find him," he promised. Then he headed straight for the window he'd previously propped open for his escape.

Mission accomplished.

CHAPTER 5

THE RAKURAI, PACIFIC OCEAN

Present Day

Tom's eyes widened, and a huge grin spread across his face. "So let me get this straight: Maldeen put you in charge of looking for *you*?"

"I know. But it was harder than it sounds," Jack said. "I had to pretend to be a Vane goon named Spellman and lead a search of the waterfront for Jack Hearn that was good enough to be believable. And Maldeen was on my tail the whole time, with his ninjas crawling everywhere. Finally we gave up, and Vane arrived. He was furious, and, good to his word, Maldeen blamed me—or I should say, he blamed Spellman. Either way, we were both as good as dead."

侍

NEW YORK CITY

Seven Weeks Ago

"Spellman, do you have any concept of how valuable Jack Hearn was to me before you let him just waltz out of the warehouse?" Vane shouted into Jack's masked face.

"Yes, sir," Jack said.

"You couldn't possibly! You can't even begin to understand the concept—how could you when you can't even complete a simple task like feeding a couple of prisoners? I should have just hired a waiter!"

"I'm . . . sorry, Mr. Vane. I'll find him. I'll bring him back to you," Jack said, trying to sound remorseful.

Beneath the mask he was sweating profusely, nervous that a sudden movement, a sudden mistake, could get him into serious trouble. Thankfully, Vane thrived on secrecy and concealment–and therefore forced his little helpers to wear ninja gear. Right now that concealment was the only thing keeping Jack alive.

Vane paced the floor. "Tell me," he said disgustedly. "Exactly how do you intend to get Jack Hearn back?"

Jack knew that the businessman would not hesitate to have him killed right then and there. Jack was sure of his own fighting abilities, but he was greatly outnumbered: There were a dozen ninjas around him, not including Vane and Maldeen. He had no chance of walking out of the warehouse alive.

"I can trap him by using his friend over there," Jack said, cocking his head in the direction of Roy's cell, but careful not to make eye contact with Roy, who was standing at the gate. Jack hoped Vane would go along with this plan, so he could get Roy out.

"You really are as thick as you look, Spellman," Vane spat. "This is Jack Hearn we're talking about. He's not going to return to the scene of the crime to rescue his friend, you dimwit."

Jack clenched his fists. There was only one thing that would get Jack Hearn to cooperate in a situation like this–and being Jack Hearn in the flesh, he knew exactly what that one thing was.

"Well, don't keep me waiting. You have all your friends at your disposal," said Vane, pointing to the other ninjas. "What's your plan?"

"I don't need any help," Jack replied. "I can do it myself. I'll go after his sons and bring them here–there's no doubt Jack Hearn will come running."

"Ah, his sons," Vane said, finally sounding somewhat pleased. "At last, an intelligent answer. I have already been keeping an eye on them. You know they have protection. . . ."

"I am . . . highly motivated," said Jack.

Vane stared at him for a moment. "Understand this: You cannot fail me. You cannot run from me. I know your every move. I am always watching."

Jack nodded and turned to go, relieved to shake off Vane and his goons for a while. But seconds later Vane uttered the words that ruined it all. "Maldeen, go with him."

Shaking his head, Jack realized that he wasn't in the clear yet. He now had to find a way to lose Maldeen, and fast. As he headed out of the warehouse, he heard Vane yell out, "Get the prisoner ready for transport, now! I don't want any more mistakes."

Jack realized that he had even less time than he'd imagined. He had to reach the boys and Jin quickly, and then get back to the warehouse before Vane moved Roy to who knows where.

As they walked, Maldeen warned Jack, "You'd better not run on me. I'm not having the boss come for me after he's done with you."

"All I want to do is get to those kids . . . but we don't have much time." Jack checked his watch. "It's a little after four, which means school has probably just let out. They'll either be home or on the subway. If we cover both, we'll have a better chance."

Maldeen looked at him. "So which one do you want to–"

"The house," Jack interrupted. He knew exactly how Maldeen operated.

Maldeen smiled. "Then that's the one *I'll* take," he said. Inside, Jack was relieved. The tough guy had taken the bait. He knew either way Maldeen would be following him, but at least this way he had permission to follow through with his plan.

"Remember, you're being watched," Maldeen reminded him.

"I won't fail," said Jack, and then he took off.

Running across town while trying to be inconspicuous was not an easy task. A couple of cops on the street eyed him suspiciously but soon decided he was harmless–they must have missed the sheathed sword hanging from his belt. When he reached the boys' subway stop along the number six train line on Lexington Avenue, he called home from a pay phone, but there was no answer.

He was too late to warn them. It was as he'd feared: He would have to launch an attack on his own children.

Maldeen and Vane would be watching his every move, of that he was sure, so he had to make it look believable. But he knew the fight would have to be short—no more than ten minutes—otherwise, his inability to harm two high-school boys would give his identity away. So Jack dialed 911 and reported a disturbance at the 51st Street subway station on the number six line. It would probably take them a while to appear on the scene, but as far as Jack was concerned, the earlier they showed up, the better. The police would complicate things, but they would ensure that "Spellman" would have only a few minutes in which to fight the boys.

Jack walked down to the subway platform, where about a dozen people were milling around, waiting for the train. A few people glanced at him, but they quickly went back to minding their own business. New Yorkers really have seen it all, Jack thought. It was a good thing it was the end of October, close enough to Halloween that he thought he might even be able to get away with pretending he was just a weird guy in a costume.

Two trains came by, but there was no sign of Tom and Mitch. Finally a third train arrived, and Jack caught sight of his sons. Relief flooded through him: The boys were okay. And they noticed him immediately.

侍

THE RAKURAI, PACIFIC OCEAN

Present Day

Laura gasped as Tom slapped the top of his head with his hands.

"So it *was* you!" Tom cried out. "You attacked us?"

"This is unreal . . . ," added Mitch, in shock.

"Boys, I'm so sorry," Jack said. "I had to make it look real. I knew Maldeen was watching me from across the platform. If I didn't look like I was really trying to take you out, he'd have sent someone else after you two. And then I wouldn't have been able to protect you. At least that way, I was the bad guy *and* the good guy. Anyway, I had called the police just before I saw you, so that the 'fight' would only have to last a few minutes."

Then Jack turned to face Laura. "But someone decided to shake things up a bit," he said, in a somewhat reprimanding tone. Then he smiled and gave her a gentle pat on the back. "Excellent work! My sons put up quite a fight, but you were terrific. I think I still feel your right elbow hook."

Laura laughed. "I never in a million years thought

I'd be commended on my fighting skills by an enemy—who turns out to be my friends' dad!"

"And I never could have dreamed that one day you'd fight my daughter, Jack!" Roy quipped.

"Honestly, if it wasn't for her, I don't think my act would have held much water. Maldeen would have known instantly that something wasn't right if Laura hadn't been there to put up a real fight. Boys, you could both learn a thing or two from her."

"Great," declared Mitch sarcastically. "First she beats me at science, and now this. . . ."

Jack and Roy began to laugh.

"Hey," Tom interjected, slightly embarrassed. "That was only our first day on the job! We've kicked Vane's butt loads of times since then."

"We can't argue with that," Jack said to Roy. "The boy has a point."

"So, Dad, what happened next?"

"Well, since I couldn't warn you about anything during the fight, I still had to warn Jin and get back to the warehouse to rescue Roy. But first I had to lose Maldeen, and whoever else Vane had watching me."

CHAPTER 6

NEW YORK CITY

Seven Weeks Ago

Jack stopped at the first pay phone he could find and called home again. This time Jin answered. "It's me," Jack said into the speaker.

Jin sounded genuinely surprised to hear from Jack. "What is the matter, Mr. Hearn? Where have you been?"

"I've just escaped from Julian Vane," Jack said quickly. "I don't know what's going on, but he'll be coming after the boys soon. Keep them safe, Jin. I'm going to rescue Roy Ting; Vane's still holding him in a warehouse on the West Side."

Jack hung up the phone, reassured that his sons were in good hands. In the eight years that Jin had been a guardian for the boys, he had never once failed Jack. He was sure Jin would provide a convincing cover for his absence. He just hoped everything would be back to normal before the boys noticed anything was awry.

Jack raced back across town, scanning the streets for any sign of Maldeen or Vane's other men. But he didn't see anyone, nor did he see any sign of Vane's guards outside the warehouse when he arrived. Suddenly a thought crossed his mind: What if he was too late?

Jack walked around the back of the warehouse until he came upon a window. Crouching down underneath it, he peeked through the window. The warehouse was completely empty! Even the cells had been removed. Roy was already on his way to whatever "paradise island" Vane had had in store for both of them.

Jack sighed. Roy was gone. And all Jack knew about this island was that it was somewhere in the Pacific—which narrowed his search to just a few hundred thousand square miles. He had no idea what his next move should be, but he knew he had to make it quickly.

What would Vane want with him and Roy Ting? Jack thought. He had no business dealings with Vane, so revenge for that purpose could be ruled out. Could Vane know that Jack and Roy were clan leaders in R.O.N.I.N.? How would he have found that out? Jack felt a sudden chill. "You are only pawns in a much larger plan," Vane had told them, but what kind of plan? If he was trying to get information out of them about someone in R.O.N.I.N., he couldn't have known too much about the organization, or he would know that clan leaders didn't really know that many other members. Did Vane have something to do with those other leaders going silent in the last few months? What game was he playing?

Knowing he couldn't solve the mystery right away, Jack decided that the first thing he had to do was get out of the ninja outfit and get somewhere safe. He changed and tossed the outfit into a bag—he had a feeling he would need to wear it again.

He would have to steer clear of home or else his sons would become more targeted than they already were.

Jack's first stop was a mini storage place downtown, where he kept some emergency supplies. Inside his unit, he found an emergency kit that included a suitcase full of clothes, cash, and various forms of different identification. For now he would be Mr. Cassidy Newby. There was also a wallet with fake family pictures and credit cards in Newby's name. None of the items could be traced to Jack Hearn, and all would hold up even under police scrutiny. He also picked up the keys to one of his clan's safe houses, and then took off.

The safe house was in the Village, busy during the day and night. It was the kind of neighborhood in which no one would stand out—the perfect place to get lost in. It was also the kind of place that Vane would never go himself, a place he wouldn't even think to search.

As Jack entered the building, a chill ran down his spine. He had not been there in years. He braced himself as he unlocked the front door.

It was a small one-bedroom apartment, spotless thanks to a cleaning service that he employed to come twice a month. He put his clothes away in a familiar old dresser and slumped on the bed.

Since Madeline had died, there were times when he felt very close to her, as if she were right by his side. The feeling was stronger here than in any other place he'd ever been. Of course, that made sense. This was, after all, the first apartment he and Madeline had shared.

Once the boys came, the place was too small for all of them, but Jack kept it. However, as with the name Cassidy Newby, an army of highly trained investigators would never be able to trace the apartment back to Jack. In the past, he meant it to be a safe place for Madeline and the boys to go in case the family was ever in danger. When she died, he'd kept it simply because he couldn't let it go.

Picking up one of the disposable cell phones he'd purchased, he called Jin.

"Mr. Hearn, are you all right?" Jin asked, with some concern in his voice.

Now that things were finally calm, Jack filled Jin in on all the details of what had happened.

"I should probably go," Jack said, once he had

THE RAKURAI, PACIFIC OCEAN . . .
THANK GOODNESS WE GOT AWAY. . . .
SO, REMEMBER THE NIGHT OF THE CITYWIDE SCIENCE FAIR?

"ROY, IT'S A SETUP!"
"YOU'RE JUST A PAWN IN A LARGER PLAN, JACK."
THAT PLAN WAS OUR ONLY HOPE. . . .

I'M SORRY, BOYS, BUT I HAD TO DO IT.
I NEEDED TO DISAPPEAR, SO I USED A NEW IDENTITY.
NEWBY
CASSIDY, M.

ONLY ONE PERSON KNEW MY WHEREABOUTS.
pop!
ストリート
THEY WERE AFTER *ME*, NOT YOU.

THANKS TO DR. GENSAI'S COMPUTER, I KNEW WHERE TO FIND VANE.
THEY WEREN'T **ALL** BLACK LOTUS. . . .
I NEEDED TO GET INSIDE SOMEHOW.

I COULDN'T BELIEVE WHAT I WAS HEARING. . . .
SIR, THE RAKURAI IS ON ITS WAY. THE HEARN BOYS ARE ON BOARD.
IT WAS CHANCE ALL ALONG. HE WAS THE TRAITOR!

FINALLY, WE'LL GET SOME ANSWERS.
THIS IS JUST LIKE IN MY DREAMS!

THOSE WEREN'T DREAMS, TOM—THEY WERE MEMORIES.
History repeats itself. A true ronin knows honor can only be restored when revenge is taken. The revenge has begun.
THE SCROLL IS GONE! WHO LEFT THIS NOTE?
ARE WE ALL THAT'S LEFT OF R.O.N.I.N.?

finished the story. "I'll be in touch."

"Take care of yourself, sir," Jin told him.

"I will," Jack replied. "Take care of the boys."

"With my life," Chance had said.

侍

THE RAKURAI, PACIFIC OCEAN

Present Day

"You know, Mr. Chance did protect us when that ninja appeared in the house later," Mitch pointed out.

"Wait, was that you too?" Tom asked, looking at Jack.

"No, but Jin told me about it," his father replied. "It was one of Vane's men. See, I knew that once 'Spellman' disappeared, you boys would be in trouble again. I knew Vane would send someone else to finish the job. I told Jin to watch out for you guys."

"I'm glad it wasn't you; that dude was way more aggressive than you were," Mitch said, relieved.

"Yeah, and he looked way more skilled," added Tom

with a laugh. "Hey, maybe you could stand to take some lessons from Laura, too."

At that, Jack burst into laughter. Tom always knew the right buttons to push for a laugh. "Remember, I wasn't actually trying to take you out on the subway platform. In fact, I was doing my best to avoid that."

"What about later, at Ting Microsystems?" Tom asked.

"That *was* me," Jack admitted. "I was keeping an eye on you boys and was very surprised to see you both head out so late—and without Mr. Chance. So of course I had to follow you. I was really impressed that you boys were able to pick up on such an important lead like Ting Microsystems so early on, barely knowing anything about what had happened to me."

"We were born with the gift," Tom announced jokingly.

"Excuse me, but *I'm* the one who led us to Laura and Ting Microsystems," Mitch reminded his brother.

"It's all about the twin frequency; how do you know *I* didn't send you that lead telepathically?" retorted Tom.

"Anyway," Jack interrupted, "the point is that you made it there. And I thought it would be my chance to get to you and fill you in on what had happened. Unfortunately, I didn't make it inside."

"That's when Mr. Chance shot you with the crossbow!" Tom said.

Jack nodded. "I didn't think anything of it at the time. He was supposed to protect you, and I was dressed like a ninja. But now I don't know what to believe."

Jack could see Mitch mulling the facts over, running them again and again through his head. "There is one thing I don't understand," Mitch said finally. "If Mr. Chance was working with Vane, why didn't he just hand us over to the guy? Or lure you in and give us all up?"

"I don't know. I'm not sure what their connection is. And I'm not sure they are always on the same side, especially after what happened later. And remember, Mr. Chance's cover was as your protector. Vane wanted me and Mr. Ting for a "larger plan." He could have been leveraging me and Mr. Ting against Chance . . . I don't know. Of course, I have my suspicions."

"I still can't believe you were gone for two months, and yet you were so close to us for so much of the time," Mitch said.

"Neither can I. But I knew I was wanted; I had to stay hidden, not only for my own safety but for yours, too. There was still a danger that Vane would try to take you at the house, and there was even one more attempt that I intercepted. I hoped that at least left Vane wondering how many Cat's Claw people were guarding you.

"I tried to learn as much as I could about Vane's plans," Jack continued. "I couldn't hack into his system, but a look at public records of purchase and shipping told me that Vane Industries had a giant construction project going on somewhere."

"Vane's Space Needle," Tom said.

Jack nodded. "I found out he was building a large complex somewhere in the Pacific, but I couldn't guess where. The only clue I had was that he wasn't buying the equipment or fuel he would need to power a place as big as he seemed to be constructing, so I guessed that he was using alternative energy sources."

"And because it was the Pacific, you thought it might be geothermal, so that led you to Dr. Gensai," Mitch concluded.

"Show-off," said Laura, punching Mitch in the arm.

"Dad, is that why you had Mr. Chance take us to Japan?" Tom asked.

"Yes, I needed to get to Japan to find Dr. Gensai and continue my investigation. Getting you out of New York and out of the reach of Vane's goons was the most important thing, and, of course, I'd still be able to keep an eye on you. I assumed that Vane would be making it to Tokyo at some point as well, but I knew there was no way he'd continue searching for you over there. The only threat I didn't factor in was the one that followed us everywhere, the one I was too blind to see."

"Mr. Chance," both boys said in unison.

CHAPTER 7

NEW YORK

Five Weeks Ago

Back at the safe house, Jack laid low for a couple of weeks, trying to determine his next step. He figured, based on the public records, that Vane would be leaving New York for this mystery island in the Pacific sometime soon, and that he would most likely spend some time in Tokyo, where he probably purchased all of his supplies and electronics. Besides, Tokyo was home to Vane's gang of Yakuza. So Jack packed his computer and the few things he would need for the trip.

Suddenly he heard the tinkling sound of wind chimes near the windows in the living room. Jack stopped in his tracks. Someone had broken into the apartment, he was sure of it. The place was well-protected by a top-of-the-line alarm system; the front door and windows were wired. But any alarm system could be compromised, and it was obvious from the sound of the chimes that someone had managed to outsmart it and enter through the window.

On the one hand, Jack had a plane to catch and didn't want to waste a lot of time on what was coming. On the other hand, he was angry that Vane had, in one simple act, desecrated the pure, innocent memories he kept of this home he'd made with Madeline so long ago.

He heard the intruder tiptoe across the hardwood floor in the living room. Taking a deep breath, Jack called through his closed bedroom door, "I'm going to give you one chance. Climb back out that window right now and you'll still have legs to walk on."

"I'll give you the same chance," Jack heard the intruder say. "Come out on your own or I'll have to carry you out."

Right, Jack thought, as he padded softly across the carpeted floor of the bedroom to a small door that stood waist-high in the wall. Many years ago it had opened to an old-fashioned dumbwaiter. Now there was just a small shaft with another door on the other side that opened into the living room.

Jack opened both doors and slipped through. This put him a few steps behind a man dressed in a black ninja outfit standing outside the bedroom door, waiting for his moment to strike.

Executing a flying front kick, Jack landed a strike to the man's back, pushing him against the door. The ninja groaned; then, even though he was dazed, he turned to face his opponent. Jack simply punched him in the jaw and the man was out cold.

Jack quickly pulled him onto the fire escape outside the window, and then he dragged the man down one flight of stairs. Back in his apartment, he called the police on his cell phone and reported that a prowler was trying to climb in a window outside the building.

Jack then finished packing and headed out the door to make his plane. During the cab ride to the airport, he realized that there was only one person who knew where he was staying: Jin Chance. He had mentioned his location to the boys' guardian earlier that day.

Jack wondered if maybe there was a tap on the home line. It seemed unlikely, but it wasn't impossible. He was glad the boys were going to Japan. Even though Vane was probably already there, for some reason Jack felt that it would still be safer than being in New York.

侍

TOKYO, JAPAN

Four Weeks Ago

"Tell Mr. Matsu it's Cas Newby; he has the number," Jack said.

"I will, and I'm sure he'll call you when he returns,"

replied the voice on the other line.

Hanging up the phone, Jack was sure something was wrong. Inoshiro Matsu wasn't just out of the office; he wasn't answering his cell phone or any of his private lines—even the one reserved for emergency communications between clan leaders. After his and Roy's recent abduction by Vane, Jack feared that something similar had happened to Inoshiro.

Of course, this complicated Jack's mission considerably. Since Roy Ting could not help him, he had been counting on assistance from the Thunderbolt Clan, of which Inoshiro was the leader. But now, if Inoshiro was also captured, it looked like Jack had to deal with Vane on his own.

Later that afternoon, Cas's cell phone rang.

"Is this Cas Newby?" asked a sweet, youthful voice.

"Yes, who is this?" Jack asked curiously.

"That's not important. Mr. Matsu has left you a package in the lobby of the Matsu Cybernetics Building. He says it is extremely important that you retrieve it immediately."

"I'll be right there."

Jack stared up at the tall glass tower of Matsu Cybernetics. The Tokyo sunlight bounced off the glass windows, illuminating the edges of the building as if it were surrounded by a halo. Jack wondered what he was about to pick up. He knew that Inoshiro didn't have anything to do with this–if there was one thing clan leaders were schooled in, it was protocol, and this could not have been further from it. Still, he was intrigued. Something in that child's voice told him this was serious; serious enough to lie about Mr. Matsu's involvement.

Back at his hotel, Jack made sure the door was locked and the hotel phone was off the hook before he opened the package–just in case. Inside, he found what looked like a comic book. It was very similar to the type of books his boys liked to read. At first he thought the book was some kind of container for something else, but he soon realized that the book was nothing other than . . . a book. There was no note, no secret compartment, no message decoder. So he sat and read the comic cover to cover. After a few read-throughs, Jack finally thought he'd figured it out.

He put the phone back on the hook to reset it, and then dialed Jin's number. The boys were about to receive their first mission.

侍

THE RAKURAI, PACIFIC OCEAN

Present Day

"So you were the one who gave Mr. Chance the *doujinshi*?" Mitch asked, amazed.

"Yup. Nikki must've found Cas Newby's information

hidden somewhere in Inoshiro's computer and decided to put me on Vane's trail," Jack added. "I must say, Nikki, that was a genius plan. Excellent work!"

"Thank you, Mr. Hearn. Your boys did a very good job of tracking down the author of the *doujinshi*, as well as tracking Vane to his island in the Pacific."

"Well, I think Brian Saito is the only one who can take credit for getting us to Vane's island," Tom said with a hint of resentment.

"Still, if Nikki hadn't put out the alert, who knows what could have happened," Jack insisted. "You knew something wasn't right with your father's avatar, Nikki, and you followed your instincts. You should be very proud of your daughter, Inoshiro."

"Indeed I am," Inoshiro stated. Nikki's cheeks blushed with happiness, though she tried hard to conceal it.

"Anyway," said Jack, continuing his story, "I checked in with Jin every now and then, but every time I asked to speak with you boys, he told me you weren't there. I figured you were just busy with the mission. The more I think about it, the more I realize how naive I was. Finally, after a few days, I decided to trail you two, to see that you were fine for myself. Jin had told me that you were going to the Shibuya District that evening. So I made it a point to be there too. Unfortunately, my plan got a bit messed up, as usual."

侍

TOKYO, JAPAN

Three Weeks Ago

Starting at the famous "scramble crossing," a busy five-way intersection that fascinated tourists, Jack wandered through the shopping district in search of Tom and Mitch. He didn't see his sons, but he noticed that most of the crowd was under twenty-five.

Most, but not all. There were a few older people, particularly two men in dark suits and sunglasses who didn't seem to care that they stood out in the crowd. . . . Jack immediately gathered that they were looking for someone—and he had a good idea who that might be.

Ducking into a coffee shop, Jack watched as the men bickered over a photo one of them was holding. He waited until after they passed the coffee shop before stepping outside and easing back into the throng—only to find himself face-to-face with a third man wearing the same dark uniform as the other two.

The man gasped as he recognized Jack, who caught a glimpse of his own face in the photograph the guy was carrying. Looking closer, Jack could see that the men were all armed. He was ready to fight but was jostled by a rowdy group of teenagers, who managed to separate him from the man who had been running toward him.

As the third guy shouted for his partners, Jack

caught sight of two blond heads in the crowd, about two hundred yards away.

Though his instinct was to fight, Jack didn't know how many of Vane's thugs were in the area. If the fight got out of control, and if Mitch and Tom saw it and tried to help him, he would never forgive himself.

Jack had only a split second to make his decision, and in the end, he turned and ran, checking once to make sure that all three thugs were following him. If he could just get them out of the crowd and away from the teenagers, he would be able to fight them.

The men began to run after Jack, and he was able to keep a reasonable lead on them as he dodged through the swarm of people in front of him. His zigzag movements took him closer to Mitch and Tom than he would have liked, but it couldn't be helped. He realized that for a moment the boys thought the thugs were after them; how he wished he could have revealed his identity to them and told them it was going to be all right. But he couldn't.

Jack ducked into an alley and leaped down a flight of stairs, crashing into a row of garbage cans at the bottom of the steps. He hoped the ruckus he caused would keep the thugs' attention on him, not on two kids riding skateboards. He hid in a doorway. After a short time, he sensed that no one was following him anymore, and he climbed back up the steps slowly.

侍

THE RAKURAI, *PACIFIC OCEAN*

Present Day

"And they were gone," Jack told the group. "Either they'd given up, which didn't seem likely, or they'd been held up."

Mitch and Tom looked at each other with quizzical looks on their faces.

"I can't believe you were right there, next to us, and we didn't know it," Tom exclaimed.

"So they were after you the whole time?" Mitch chimed in. "And we thought they were after us. Of course, when they just vanished like that, we started to think maybe they weren't."

Jack nodded. "Well, what were you supposed to

think? You had your eyes open, and your instincts were right on."

Tom smiled. "Too bad we couldn't have been there when they went back to Vane empty-handed."

"Actually, given what I know, I don't think they were Vane's men," Jack said.

"Whose were they?" asked Tom.

"Mr. Chance's . . . ," Mitch guessed, something finally clicking in his head.

"Well, at the time I thought they were Vane's–it made sense," Jack said. "He had tried to take me before. But then I keep coming back to two things: One, Vane had said that Roy and I were just pawns in a larger game. That meant Vane wasn't the only one in charge here, and he was using us to flex his muscles. And two, Chance was the only one who knew I was in Japan, let alone Shibuya."

"Maybe it was like you said, someone hacked into Mr. Chance's cell phone or something," Tom suggested.

"That's what I thought. Believe me, boys, the idea that Jin Chance was an enemy hadn't even occurred to me at that point. So, to test his phone, I called Jin again. I didn't tell him what had just happened, but I told him that I had switched hotels and would now be staying in a particular room in a hotel in Shibuya. Three hours later I watched from across the street as more men in suits and sunglasses stormed the room. Now I was sure that talking to Jin wasn't safe."

"But maybe the phone was tapped," Tom repeated, still not quite convinced that Mr. Chance would betray his family.

"You're right, Tom. At that point, all that call did was prove that the phone had been compromised. That's why I continued to trust him. I just didn't tell him anything about where I was or what I was doing. On the other hand, I didn't tell him about my suspicions, either. Come to think of it, Jin tried to get my whereabouts out of me every time I called. He told me he'd gotten a new phone, debugged it, etc., but I still didn't want to trust the connection."

"So all you knew was that the phone was tapped. But you still attacked Mr. Chance," Mitch began to say.

"I did. The proof came later," Jack revealed.

CHAPTER 8

"I had been operating on my own," Jack continued, "but it was still tough to accept that it was no longer safe to talk to the only person I had direct contact with, the person I had relied on for more than a decade. I decided that Japan had gotten too dangerous for you boys and told Jin to take you home. He had told me that you guys reached a dead end with the *doujinshi*, and I didn't press for more information. I just wanted you to get home safely. I didn't tell him where I was, only that I would join you all shortly. He agreed."

"Chance never mentioned going home," Mitch said, as Tom shook his head.

"Well, that's not surprising now. Whatever he was up to, he used you two as a cover. As long as you thought you were on a mission that I supported–and perhaps disappeared trying to complete–you would do whatever he told you. At the same time, he could direct you to the places he needed to be.

"Anyway, thinking you were on your way to safety, my next step was to get to Dr. Gensai," Jack went on. "I hoped he could tell me the location of Vane Island. I knew that in the long run, the only way we'd be completely safe was if I took the fight to Vane. When I got to the lab, Gensai was gone. And not just gone, but he had disappeared. I managed to hack into his records and found out that he hadn't made a withdrawal, paid a bill, or used any credit cards in some time.

"I knew then that Vane had him, and Dr. Gensai's computer told me where—at least it told me that Dr. Gensai had surveyed a number of islands in the Pacific for a big geothermal project. He had a short list, and I cross-checked it with public records to find that only one of them had been earmarked to receive extremely large shipments of concrete. Now I knew where Dr. Gensai and Roy were being held. For the first time since this whole thing started in a parking garage, I felt like I was ahead of Vane. So I took what I needed from the computer and then jammed it up with some kind of bug. Then I trashed the lab and went off to find a boat to get me to the island."

"Actually, you didn't trash everything. Mr. Chance found a map in the lab," Mitch told his father. "And Dr. Gensai had a backup disk stored in a special compartment in the computer. It's a good thing *we* found it and no one else did."

Jack nodded. "Well, it turns out it was a good thing I got sloppy, considering the kind of damage you boys did on the island."

"Think about what we could have done if you'd let us in on everything," said Tom.

Jack smiled. "You're right. I was so caught up in getting you away from danger, I didn't think about that. And I still didn't know the truth about Jin, though I started to get an idea. . . ."

侍

TOKYO, JAPAN

Three Weeks Ago

Jack was about to check out of his hotel. Picking up his suitcase and laptop, he waited for the elevator to take him down to the lobby. When the elevator door opened, two men stepped out and blocked the doorway so that Jack could not get on. They were wearing the same uniform as the men in Shibuya a few days before: business suits and sunglasses.

Jack immediately knew he wouldn't be checking out of the hotel right away. He'd fight if he had to, but in the narrow space of the hallway, the fight would quickly turn into a grappling match. And two trained men would get the better of him sooner or later.

It was time for plan B. Jack turned and was about to run down the hallway in the other direction and head for the stairs. At that moment, though, the stairway door opened and two more men stepped out. They recognized him immediately; these men were wearing Vane's Black Lotus ninja uniform.

Jack realized that things had just gotten worse. He was now trapped between the two pairs of warring thugs. He knew why Vane's men were after him, but who did these suits answer to? He tried to scan their faces and bodies for any signs or symbols that might give them away. All he could make out was what looked like a lotus flower tattoo on the inside wrist of one of the suits. Jack's eyes widened at this; suddenly, certain things started to make sense. He realized then what Vane meant when he said they were just pawns in a larger plan—this was some kind of coup scheme to take over R.O.N.I.N. There had been rumors about something of this nature for decades, but no one ever paid them any mind. It was all just a legend, they had said; there was never any evidence to back anything up.

Suddenly the men moved in on him. Jack had no choice; he let himself back into his room and locked the door behind him. He hoped that maybe the two pairs would just take each other out and forget all about him.

A moment later he heard shouting and the sounds of a struggle. His wish had come true.

Peering through the peephole, Jack watched fists,

feet, and bodies go flying as the men fought one another. After hearing three bodies fall to the ground, Jack took his cue and opened the door. He rushed for the only thug who was still conscious. The man looked up in surprise as Jack's combination of strikes caught him in the face. The man went down.

侍

THE RAKURAI, PACIFIC OCEAN

Present Day

"A lotus flower? Was it white?" the boys said together.

"Yes! You know the symbol?" said Jack in surprise.

"Yeah, one of Mr. Chance's friends at the Sea of Trees had the mark. We assumed it was the symbol of another R.O.N.I.N. clan," Tom explained.

Jack let out a sigh; this was his biggest fear realized.

"I don't know who the White Lotus are, but they aren't R.O.N.I.N. Over the years, certain rumors about a rogue clan have spread through the organization.

Apparently, when your grandfather was the leader of Cat's Claw, after R.O.N.I.N. had first reformed, the Lotus Clan became known to all as being aggressive and power-hungry; they always seemed to want more fame and prestige than the Dragon thought was appropriate. Remember, we are R.O.N.I.N. to make the world a better place, not for the glory. Anyway, the rumors continued, and they became more and more elaborate over time. Some members heard that the Lotus Clan had started its own secret organization, and that when we least expected it, the Lotus Clan would strike against the rest of us. It has been more than fifty years since these rumors began, and nothing has ever come of them. We just wrote them off as you would an old wives' tale—until now. It's no coincidence that the two groups of men who have been trying to kill me have tattoos of Black and White Lotus. Someone may be trying to recreate a past legend, or else they've been plotting a coup for a very long time. Either way, it seems that Jin Chance and Julian Vane somehow wound up on warring sides of the rogue Lotus Clan, and it became divided into Black and White. But I get the sense that neither one of them is really in charge. They're answering to someone else."

"Who?" the boys asked eagerly.

"I don't know yet, but I have my suspicions. Besides,

I'm getting ahead of myself here. First I owe you the final bit of incriminating evidence against Jin. I found it on Vane Island."

"When did you get to the island, anyway?" Tom asked his father.

"About a week before you did," Jack said. Then, looking at Roy, he added, "Since I was dressed as a Black Lotus ninja, I was able to move about freely on the island. None of the other ninjas ever suspected I wasn't really one of them; at least if they did, they didn't let on. I just had to stay away from Vane and that Maldeen guy. I never saw Maldeen, though; I guess he stayed behind in New York."

"What did you do while you were there?" asked Mitch.

"I surveyed the island and tried to figure out how to get everyone out—Roy, Dr. Gensai, Inoshiro . . . The problem was that while I had freedom on the island, all transportation off the island was watched very carefully. And even though I was supposedly a ninja, getting in and out of the prison was strictly watched as well."

"All while you were on your own," Roy added.

Jack nodded. "I knew it wouldn't be easy, but I found out that the prison was the least of our problems."

侍

VANE ISLAND, PACIFIC OCEAN

One Week Ago

Though Jack could move freely around the island, he didn't dare enter the Vane Needle. As much as he disliked Vane, Jack had to admit that the building was . . . well, cool. Almost identical—at least on the outside—to the Space Needle in Seattle, Vane's building was more than five hundred feet tall. The top of the building was a large saucer, several floors thick, supported by a cylinder that sat on a tremendous reinforced concrete base.

Jack had taken the boys to the actual Space Needle, and he thought that Vane's engineers had done a remarkable job of re-creating it here. And judging by the size of the geothermal generator and the amount of high-end digital communications equipment moving into it, the building was about to become one of the biggest and most powerful communications command and control centers in the world—unless Jack had something to say about it. And he intended to have plenty to say. Vane would only have created something like this if he was planning something that would cause a great deal of harm, of this Jack was certain. He was also fairly sure that this island somehow played into Vane's bigger scheme—the one in which he intended to use all the R.O.N.I.N. prisoners as pawns—and there was no way Jack was going to let that happen.

Whatever Vane's plans were, his secrets were in the building. Jack knew he had to get inside, and soon. He had to rescue Roy, Inoshiro, Dr. Gensai . . . and until Jack had completed this mission, he could not go home to his boys.

After watching for a while, Jack was able to time how often ninjas entered and left the building, how many went in at a time, and what entrances they came and left from. After sufficient research, he decided to try entering through the subbasement, the least-used exit.

Slipping in at night, he hid behind the large compressors that ran the building's air-conditioning system. The equipment was state-of-the-art and designed to run with a small maintenance crew, so it was easier for Jack to make sure he wouldn't run into anyone. He found a computer terminal near the air-conditioning control panel. There was only simple security on the system because the terminal was hooked up just to the air unit—no other systems or machines. Under normal circumstances, this would have been considered a wise move by Vane, but since Jack was only interested in the layout of the facility, the terminal showed him everything he needed to know: the complete blueprints for the building's ventilation system.

Jack located a route to the penthouse floor of the needle. He would need to climb up the elevator shaft and enter the walls through the air vents. Using the ladder in the elevator shaft, Jack climbed the nearly five hundred feet to the bottom of the saucer at the top of the needle. There, he entered the ventilation system and followed the route he'd memorized to Vane's office. The shaft was tight, and he had to move slowly, but he was able to manage it.

Finally, by the early morning, Jack had made his way into the duct that terminated in Vane's office. When Vane arrived a short time later, there was nothing standing between the two men but a metal grill and some oxygen. Jack was very still and waited for something to happen. Fortunately, he didn't have to wait long.

A man entered the office. Vane didn't even bother to look up. "What is it, Baxter?" he asked in a bored tone.

"The *Rakurai* is on its way," Baxter replied.

Vane's attitude suddenly changed. "Excellent!" he exclaimed. "Chance and the Hearn boys are onboard?"

Jack was shocked. It took every ounce of self-control he had to keep still and not give himself away. What he was hearing was impossible! Jin and the boys should have been home by now, waiting in a safe house until Jack arrived. Jack did not want to believe what Baxter had just reported, but he knew that it was obviously true. Somehow Jin, Mitch, and Tom had not gone home and would soon be on Vane Island. Jack felt a cold dread in his stomach. There were only a few possible explanations for how this could have happened, and Jack was sure he wouldn't like any of them.

"And there's more, Mr. Vane. Our source has told us that the Ting girl is onboard as well," Baxter said with pride.

"Fine, fine," Vane said dismissively. "She can rot in a cell with her father, but Chance . . ."

Vane grew thoughtful. "He's been a thorn in my side for too long. And his arrogance! He's been bending and scraping in the house of Hearn and his brats for years, just to feed information upstairs. And for what? If he thinks I'm going down without a fight, he is sorely mistaken. Oh yes, the gods favor the bold, Baxter. I'll accomplish more in one day than Chance has done in years of his foolish game of pretend. And then everyone will know who the real boss is. Let me know when they arrive—I'll want to greet them personally."

Jack had to physically steady himself. Suddenly it all made sense. No one was tapping into his communications with Jin; Jin himself was the leak—a traitor to him, to his boys, and to his clan. The two suits with the White Lotus mark in the hotel must have been Chance's men—the very same ones who'd chased him down in the Shibuya District and broke into the hotel Jack lied about being at. Jin Chance was trying to capture him before Vane could. But what was the ultimate endgame? Whose attention were they fighting for?

Jack was outraged. He had inducted Jin into his own clan, trusted him with the lives of his sons. And all the while Jin had been working for someone else, gathering information, biding his time, putting the Hearn family in danger. Jack would have to put a stop to it, but first he had to rescue his sons.

CHAPTER 9

THE RAKURAI, PACIFIC OCEAN

Present Day

The boys listened raptly and were silent at the end. Finally Tom spoke. "See, I told you, the ventilation shaft should have worked."

"What?" asked Laura.

"The shaft–I knew it was a way out," Tom said.

"What do you mean?" Jack asked.

"When we were trying to get out of Vane's office, I tried to use the shaft, probably the same one you did, but there were these inserts inside, making the opening too small."

"That one's on me, I'm afraid. In my effort to make it out of there alive, I think I may have damaged one of the sides of the vent, forcing it to slide down halfway and virtually blocking the vent."

"So how could you face Mr. Chance after hearing

all of this, without revealing how you felt?" Laura wondered aloud, bringing the conversation back to the matter at hand.

"I was glad I had the ninja mask," said Jack thoughtfully. "Otherwise, it would have been impossible."

侍

VANE ISLAND, PACIFIC OCEAN

Two Days Ago

Jack made his way down the elevator shaft ladder and back to solid ground. Still shaking from what he'd overheard, he managed to find refuge behind a row of bushes and camped out there for the night. He wanted to be alert and on the scene when the *Rakurai* pulled up to the shore.

The next morning Jack awoke to see the *Rakurai* already docked. He watched Vane's ninjas lining up Tom, Mitch, and Laura and tying them up with chains. His stomach sank, and he felt nauseous. They're just kids, he thought to himself. Who could be so cruel? He was preparing to follow the boys when out of the corner of his eye, he noticed Jin Chance slinking off in the opposite direction. Jack immediately changed his target direction. Jin wasn't getting away from him–that Jack vowed. No matter what it took, that traitor's gig was finally up.

Jack trailed Jin slowly and carefully; the last thing he needed was to be discovered before the boys and prisoners were safely off the island. He needed to do everything strategically, no matter how hard it was to keep his emotions at bay. He followed Jin all the way to the back of the island, in the complete opposite direction of the needle. He didn't know exactly where Jin was going, but Jin looked as though he had a definitive plan—a pointed and dangerous one, no doubt. Jack watched as Jin entered what looked like a small steel hut on top of a hill, surrounded by nothing but barren land. Jack surmised that there was some kind of computer terminal or command system inside, though he couldn't know for sure. What worried him more was how determined Jin looked, and what kind of disaster his determination would bring upon them all.

Once Jin emerged, Jack waited to make sure he was gone before going in after him. Just as Jack was about to enter, Jin appeared on the other side of the door. Obviously, Jin had sensed someone was on his tail. For a moment they stared at each other with pure hatred. Of course, Jack was still wearing a Black Lotus ninja outfit, and Jin had no way of knowing that the person inside the mask was not one of Vane's goons. Jack thought of taking Jin out then and there, but he decided against it. It was too risky, too selfish. He needed to set his anger aside and save the others before he could seek revenge.

"Jin!" Jack cried out, as he pulled the mask off to reveal his true identity. He was trying hard to fake his shock. The less Jin knew about what Jack had learned, the better. It would be tough, but Jack needed to act like nothing between them had changed. "What are you doing here?"

"Mr. Hearn," Jin called out, with little surprise in his tone.

"What's going on? Why didn't you take the boys home like I told you?"

"They would not go home without you, sir. They insisted that we follow some leads. I tried to reason with them, but you know how they can be. I thought as long as I was there to protect them, they would be okay. Most of the time we spent on the sea and out of danger."

"Well, Jin, I am disappointed. I wanted the boys away from danger. Where are they now?"

"They are with Vane. I was just trying to find a map of the island, to figure out the best route to them. Now that you are here, they have a chance of escaping. Shall we go rescue them?"

It took every ounce of restraint inside Jack to keep him from tackling Jin to the ground. But he knew this would do him no good. As long as Jin was keeping up this little game, he would too. There had to be a reason why Jin wasn't revealing himself yet, and as long as he was still fighting on their side, the boys, Laura, and even the prisoners had a chance. So Jack took a deep breath and looked back at Jin with the biggest fake grin he could muster.

"Let's go get our boys."

侍

THE RAKURAI, PACIFIC OCEAN

Present Day

"You know the rest," Jack finished. "Jin and I helped you at the prison and in the escape from the island. Once you were all safely on board the ship, I did what I had to do with him."

"Wait," cried Mitch, "do you think Mr. Chance set off the self-destruct in that metal hut you saw him in?"

"Yes, Mitch, I do. At the time I didn't know what it was, but once I heard the announcement I knew for sure it was him. I think he had plans to let the island devour all of us and escape on the *Rakurai* by himself. Though, as it turns out, his plan didn't really work."

"But if he planned to just escape on his own," Tom said, "then why did he go to all that trouble to help us and save everyone else?"

"I'm not sure, Tom. That's a good question. Maybe he didn't intend to leave alone. Maybe he just wanted to destroy Vane and keep the rest of us R.O.N.I.N. for his own boss. In fact, that seems much more likely, now that I think about it."

"You are right, Jack," concluded Roy. "There is definitely something going on. Something is threatening the security of R.O.N.I.N., and now that we know that the rumors of the Lotus Clan are true, I think we must assume those of the Black Dragon are as well."

"What? Who's the Black Dragon? I thought there was only one leader of R.O.N.I.N.," said Tom.

"There is," Jack replied. "Just hang in there, I'm getting to that, I promise." Then he turned to face Inoshiro. "How soon will we be at Dragon Island?"

"In about ten minutes," Inoshiro answered.

"We're almost there. I think we'll know a lot more once we get there," Jack told his sons.

"It'll be so weird to finally see the place I've been dreaming about," Tom said.

"What dreams, Tom? You've been dreaming about Dragon Island?" asked Jack.

Tom told Jack all about the dreams he'd been having about the island, the jade dragon statue, the Dragon Scroll, and the men arriving with guns.

Jack groaned. "Are you sure that's what you saw?"

Tom nodded his head. "Positive. I've been seeing it over and over for weeks."

"Oh no, Roy. I think it's worse than we even imagined."

"Worse?" the boys and Laura chimed in at once.

"Yes. Before I tell you what I'm thinking, I want to talk to the two people on this boat who worked directly for Vane."

"Kunio, did Vane talk about any conflict with other organizations or mention any names of someone he either answered to or wanted to take revenge on?"

"I don't know if it was related to any problem between the Black Lotus and the White Lotus, but he was planning something, something he didn't want his boss to know about," Kunio said. "The island was only part of it, but he never told me anything. I was just a lowly kid who he ordered around." Kunio sounded slightly ashamed.

"Did he ever mention who this boss was?" Jack asked.

"Vane called his boss Rosso, but that's all I know," said Kunio.

"Roy," asked Jack, "does that name mean anything to you?"

"No, but it could be a code of some kind," Roy said.

Next Jack went to get Nadia. He was impressed that she didn't seem intimidated when she entered the room. Of course, getting her to cooperate might be a different matter.

"We have some questions for you about Vane, Nadia," Jack said. "He was part of something I can't give you all of the details about, but I think it's something very dangerous and very serious."

"I owe Vane nothing; just ask what you want to know."

"Did he ever mention the name of a superior, a boss of any kind?" Jack asked.

"Well, a few time I did see some fax that came and had a signature of R.O.B.D.," said Nadia.

Jack and Roy exchanged looks of surprise.

"Did Vane ever refer to this person by name?" Jack asked.

"No, not that I hear," Nadia replied.

"Did Vane ever mention the name Rosso?"

Nadia shook her head. "No."

"Thank you, Nadia," Jack said, and indicated that she could leave.

"So who is the Black Dragon, and who is Rosso?" Mitch asked, once Nadia had left the room.

"No one knows, but like the rumors of the rogue Lotus Clan, every R.O.N.I.N. clan leader has heard of the Black Dragon at one time or another . . . although we're not really sure if he exists," said Jack, looking at both Roy and Inoshiro.

"Huh?" Tom said.

"You know who the Dragon is, the person who revived R.O.N.I.N. and created the organization we now belong to," Jack explained. "A few years after the creation of the modern R.O.N.I.N. organization, stories of a Black Dragon began to travel among the member circles and clans. He was called the Black Dragon because he was said to oppose the ideals that the Dragon held near and dear.

"But it was hard to tell if the stories were true; no one knew anything for sure, and again, we thought these tales were just ghost stories to keep us on our toes."

"Just like with our Dragon, though, if the Black Dragon did exist, he wouldn't tell too many people his identity or his location, for his own protection, right?" Laura said.

"Yes, if the Black Dragon does exist, then it would make sense that he would be protected in the same way we protect our Dragon," Jack agreed.

"So are you saying that Vane could be working for the Black Dragon? Or is he working for Rosso? Or are they the same guy?" Mitch asked.

"We don't have all the facts, but that would fit what we know. It also would tie into something Roy and I have been concerned about for some time. You all know that secrecy is an important part of what we do as R.O.N.I.N. Though there are forty-seven clans, each clan leader knows only a handful of other clan leaders. The only person with the entire list is the Dragon, who keeps the master Scroll, the Dragon Scroll. This protects the other clans if one clan is destroyed or compromised. Even if one clan member or leader is captured, he can only reveal a handful of others."

"Unless the Dragon or the Scroll is captured," Tom said. "Then everyone is at risk."

"Exactly. We need the Dragon for coordination of the clans, but if the Dragon was ever captured by one of the rogue Lotus clans, or by the Black Dragon, then all clans would be in danger," said Jack.

"Well, that's why we're going to Dragon Island, isn't it? That's what my dreams have been showing me! The Scroll is in danger, and we need to get there and save it before it's too late!" Tom cried.

"Excuse me, Jack," called Inoshiro from the other side of the deck. "I think there's something you should see."

Jack got up and walked over to Inoshiro, who was preparing to steer the boat near the shore. They had finally arrived at Dragon Island; this was the moment of truth.

"What is it, Inoshiro? Is everything all right?"

"I don't know. While you were continuing your story, I went below deck to search for anything that Mr. Chance might have left behind, to see if maybe he left some clues."

"Good thinking. So you found something?"

"Yes, I did." Inoshiro handed Jack a tattered piece of paper that had been folded four times. On one side of the folded paper was written in red ink: "URGENT. In the event of my death, give to Jack Hearn."

"I did not open it," Inoshiro continued, "but I thought you should see it at once."

"Thank you very much," Jack said quietly, unable to take his eyes off the unmistakable handwriting. He couldn't believe that Jin had been keeping this from him for all these years. But then again, he thought, why should this surprise me? Jin was my enemy, plain and simple.

Seeing that note opened up so many old wounds and unleashed so many horrible possibilities for the truth of a past he had already made peace with.

"Dad, what is it?" Mitch asked, as his father made his way to the front of the deck in a slight daze.

"Where did that come from?" Tom asked.

"Mr. Matsu found it in some of Jin's things that he left behind. He's apparently been hanging on to this letter for a very long time—seven years, to be exact."

"Seven years!" cried Tom. "That must be some important letter. Who's it from?"

"It's from your grandfather. It looks like he wrote it to me the year he died."

CHAPTER 10

"So open it," said Mitch.

"I can't believe it," echoed Tom. "Mr. Chance had it the whole time! How did he get it?"

"Tom, I'm not sure I want to know the answer to that," Jack said. "But we can't focus on this now. We've arrived at our destination. We need to go find what we came all this way for. We'll read it later."

Tom and Mitch exchanged looks; they didn't understand how their father could take the suspense, but neither one of them wanted to pry. Tom looked out at the island and had an incredible sense of déjà vu, as if he had seen this place before. Of course, he had . . . in his dreams.

"That's it, that's exactly like I dreamed it," he said excitedly. "This is what I've seen, Dad."

His father put a hand on his shoulder and said, "Come on, let's go."

They launched the skiff, which was a remarkably fast dual-engine boat, and headed for the island. The edges of the island were mostly sheer drops, and they had to circle before they found a safe place to approach. Finally they found a narrow passage that seemed to be carved out of the rock. Inoshiro carefully piloted the boat toward the interior of the island. The passage opened up, and then there was an old but sturdy-looking dock that led to a small beach. Once they'd tied up the boat at the dock, Tom felt an unmistakable chill.

"Dad, we have to be careful. In my dreams, there were dozens of men with guns. . . . ," he said.

"I know; we'll be careful. But there are no other ships here–I think we'll be okay," said Jack calmly. "Which way should we go?"

Tom was only a little surprised that he knew exactly where to lead everyone. Stepping ahead, he found a path through the brush and headed toward the mountain.

The air was thick with anticipation. Everyone was

quiet, deep in their own thoughts, as the R.O.N.I.N. members climbed up the side of the mountain. After a while, they were almost at the top. There, as in his dream, Tom saw an opening in the rock . . . it was a cave. Above the entrance was another object from his dream: a large Japanese dragon carved out of jade, with bright, emerald green eyes. It looked like a guardian, standing watch over the cave.

"Stop," Jack called out to his son. "Roy, Inoshiro, and I will take the lead."

Turning on his flashlight, Jack had the others do the same as they entered the cave. A few torches lined the walls. The adults lit each one, giving them extra light. They walked along the rocky path, heading downward and deeper into the mountain. The cave finally emptied out into a large round chamber with a solid jade floor. There were symbols carved on the floor: a crane, a thunderbolt, a cat's claw . . . forty-seven symbols in all, one for each of the clans.

"Do you know where the Scroll is?" Inoshiro asked Tom.

Tom nodded. He walked through the narrow paths of the cave, now brightly lit with torches and flashlights. Not once did Tom hesitate, wondering which way to turn. His dreams about the island had been so vivid. It was as though a map of the place had been burned into his memory.

This is it, Tom thought as he turned the corner, into the nook where the Scroll was kept. He approached the pedestal and reached out to grab the rolled-up piece of parchment that was sitting in the dragon's iron claws atop the pedestal.

"Dad, it's here!" he cried out in relief. "We made it!"

Jack came closer, but could tell from where he had been standing that the piece of parchment was definitely not the Scroll.

"Actually, son, that isn't the Scroll. I don't know what it is, but the Scroll is long gone."

Everyone was silent. The adults were quiet, mourning over a fear they knew had finally come to pass; and the teenagers were silent out of sheer disbelief.

"But my visions . . . ," Tom whispered. "So you're saying that actually happened? But how did I see the men take it in my dreams? Men in black suits with guns. How did I know that?"

"Those weren't dreams, Tom, they were memories. You were here when they took it," Jack said. "And so were you, Mitch. I wanted to see if the dreams were actually true before I told you. See, you boys were initiated into R.O.N.I.N. when you were seven years old, right here in this very cave, a few months before your mother died. During the initiation ceremony, you were given the mark of your clan—the tattoos you wear. You weren't supposed to remember anything, either of you. You were supposed to go through the ritual hypnosis that takes place after initiation . . . for the protection of the clan, the organization, the island–"

"So that means I've been here too?" Laura asked her dad.

"Yes," Roy replied. "We have all been here. But for some reason, Tom still carries memories of his initiation that include the Scroll being stolen."

"My hunch is that neither Tom nor Mitch was hypnotized, because the Dragon wasn't around to do it. Whoever took the Scroll must have known where the drop-off was for Tom and Mitch, and when I picked them up, everything seemed like it was going according to plan. Maybe the trauma of the experience made you block it out," Jack added, turning to face Mitch, "whereas your brother couldn't block it. I don't know."

Turning to Jack and Inoshiro, Roy said, "It is up to us to find out what's going on, to find the Dragon . . . and the Scroll."

Looking at the puzzled expressions of the younger R.O.N.I.N. members, Jack elaborated. "If the Dragon Scroll is gone, it can only mean that the Dragon himself has been taken."

"Vane. Vane was here that night the Scroll was taken," Tom announced. "I've seen his face in my dreams. He was at the island. He took the Dragon."

"Well, that's a good start, son, but we can't assume he was working alone. Not anymore. We already know he answers to at least one leader. And Jin Chance fits into this plan somewhere, somehow."

"Wait, open that!" cried Laura, pointing to the roll of parchment still in Tom's hand.

Tom carefully unrolled the piece of paper, which bore the watermark of the lotus flower on its back. The paper was large for a note so succinct. He read it aloud to the others.

"'History repeats itself. A true ronin knows honor can only be restored when revenge is taken. The revenge has begun.' Signed with some strange signature stamp that I can't make out. What is this?" he asked, showing the scroll to Inoshiro.

"The Japanese letters are read vertically," Inoshiro explained to everyone. "I think the stamp says R.O.B.D."

There was a moment of silence as everyone realized the gravity of the situation. They all replayed the last conversation they'd had aboard the *Rakurai* before they docked. Were the legends and ghost stories all true? Did they have all those years to prevent this, but instead just turned a blind eye?

"Wait–if the Scroll has been taken, that means

someone knows all the members of the forty-seven clans and their locations," surmised Nikki.

"Which means . . . for all we know, the other clans may have all been taken out," Mitch added grimly. "If the scroll was taken when we were seven, they've had a long time to plot the demise of R.O.N.I.N."

"Are you saying *we* may be all that's left of R.O.N.I.N.?" asked Laura, unwilling to believe that this might be true.

No one had an answer for her.

"So what do we do now?" asked Mitch.

"Find out who the bad guys are and kick their butts?" Tom suggested.

"I think that's a pretty good place to start," Jack replied, patting his sons' backs.

"So, what about that note from our grandfather? Are you going to read it?" Mitch asked his father.

"Right, I almost forgot," Jack said, unfolding the letter halfway and reading it first to himself and then aloud. "'Jack, by the time this finds you, you'll already know that I am no longer alive. What you don't know is that Madeline was killed. R.O.N.I.N. is in danger. I wish I had the answers, but unfortunately, this is all I managed to gather. Follow my leads and save R.O.N.I.N. Please know that I love you and am sorry I have to leave this burden on your shoulders. Send the boys my love.

Your loving father, Frank.'"

"Mom was killed!" the boys shouted in unison.

There was silence in the cave as the boys fell to the ground, shocked by what they'd just heard. "I can't believe it," Tom said. "She was killed because of this? This rogue clan and this Scroll?" Tom was angry and confused. Mitch was just speechless.

"I'm so sorry, boys; I didn't want to believe it was possible, but your grandfather was never wrong. His instincts were what I admired most about him. Even the Dragon had his suspicions; in fact, that was the whole reason Jin Chance became your guardian in the first place: The Dragon wanted someone trained to watch over you after Madeline's death. He felt there was something unsettling about it, but I didn't want to listen."

"What is on the other side of the letter?" Roy asked, pointing to the back.

"It looks like a timeline, and a list of some leads."

"Well, we'd better get crackin', right, Dad?" Mitch asked.

Jack looked around the cave at all the friendly faces and managed a partial smile. "Right, son," he said.

As the R.O.N.I.N. members made the sad walk out of the cave back to the ship in silence, it became clear that nothing would ever be the same.

DYLAN SPROUSE AND COLE SPROUSE ARE TWO OF HOLLYWOOD'S MOST EMINENT RISING STARS.

Dylan and Cole were born in Arezzo, Italy, and currently reside in Los Angeles, California. Named for the jazz singer and pianist Nat King Cole, Cole's list of favorites includes math, the color blue, and animals. He also enjoys video games and all types of sports, including motocross, snowboarding, and surfing. Dylan, named after the poet Dylan Thomas, is very close to his brother and also has a great love of animals and video games. He enjoys science, the Los Angeles Lakers, and the color orange. He's a sports enthusiast and especially loves motocross, snowboarding, surfing, and basketball.

Cole and Dylan made their acting debuts on the big screen in *Big Daddy*, opposite Adam Sandler. Both also starred in *The Astronaut's Wife*, *Master of Disguise*, and *Eight Crazy Nights*. On television Cole and Dylan established themselves in the critically acclaimed ABC comedy series *Grace Under Fire* and eventually went on to star in NBC's *Friends* as David Schwimmer's son, Ben Geller.

Dylan and Cole currently star as the introspective Cody Martin and the mischievous Zack Martin, respectively, in the Disney Channel's amazingly successful sitcom *The Suite Life of Zack and Cody*, playing separate roles for the first time. Ranked number one in its time slot against all basic cable shows, *The Suite Life* is now one of the Disney Channel's top shows and is rapidly gaining worldwide success.

In September 2005 the Sprouses partnered with Dualstar Entertainment Group to launch the *Sprouse Bros.* brand, the only young men's lifestyle brand designed by boys for boys. The brand includes *Sprouse Bros. 47 R.O.N.I.N.*, an apparel collection, an online fan club, mobile content, a DVD series in development, and lots more in the works!